The shine of sorrowful youth

the shine *of* sorrowful youth (a novel)

Asaf Amit

Translated by Yardenne Greenspan

Polysemy literary press

For Mika

"Of all the stars, there must be far away

A single star which still exist apart."

Rainer Maria Rilke

When I got back down to the lobby of the building on Carmel Mount, carrying the measuring kit I had forgotten in the car, Shahar was nowhere to be found. Whenever I accompanied him to survey a property, especially those aging apartments destined for demolition, I often wondered if his imagination delved deep enough to contemplate the inherent dysphoria of mapping a fragment of life that would soon cease to exist.

No doubt, he was already engrossed in the work we were here to do. I climbed up the steps, gripping the railing as if using it to propel my body upwards, with no intention of loosening my hand from this remnant of another time. I knew this very kind of railing was made of bent iron pipe. I knew the area, too, and I knew the pair of twin buildings. They were identical in their stature, their paint jobs, and the square apertures in the walls alongside the balconies. But this building had open balconies, while those on the building across the way, where my grandmother used to live, were enclosed with shutters.

It was up similarly worn stairs as these that I was, once upon a time, carried on a gurney to my grandmother's apartment on the fourth floor. I was eleven years old, and at the end of each flight of stairs, as they turned left on the landing, the medics were forced to raise the gurney up above the railing, lifting it over their shoulders.

I reached the second-floor landing and heard Shahar's determined footfalls one story above, his measuring stick dragging on the floor behind him. I hurried up the stairs. As I reached him, Shahar made one polite tap, then knocked his fist against the door with the assertiveness of a battering ram. While he raised a racket, I located the electric bell beside the door and pressed it with vain tenacity, but the bell sank into the wall plate with a hollow click.

"Hold on … hold on!" a hoarse cry rose from within, as if from the bottom of a deep well, before the door opened. The elderly tenant's flushed face attested to the fact that the loud knocking had bulldozed his responses. Whenever he tried to speak, a severe cough spewed from his dry throat, shattering his words.

"My grandson came by yesterday and prepared the place," he finally managed. He gestured meekly toward the living room, his hand, though trembling, lingering in midair. He seemed to have forgotten its existence as he sought out his next thought and unsteadily showed us into his home.

A low oval table stood at the center of the living room, and a short couch with two matching armchairs, all with wooden armrests and rough plaid upholstery, were set at some distance from the walls. The old man begged our forgiveness and said the place was now at our disposal. If we needed anything, he would be sitting right over there, reading. He opened a book and then shut it around his finger, using it as a bookmark, and took small steps toward the armchair. Turning his back on the chair, he slowly reversed until his feet bumped against it, and he plopped down into a seated position.

In the meantime, Shahar was leaning his measuring stick against the wall and pinning a crisp new sheet of graph paper to his clipboard. He scanned the space around him as I pulled my measuring tools from their case. We spent a little time measuring the narrow kitchen and the living room, circling the old man who had lost himself in his book, as if he were alone and undisturbed. Then, we walked deeper into the apartment to measure the hallway and bedrooms. When we returned to the living room, the tenant raised his brows and reminded us about the balcony, whose glass doors were concealed by long, thick drapes.

It was only in the midst of our measuring assignment, as I glanced out the window of his bedroom at the neighboring building and its enclosed balconies, that I knew for certain this was the apartment where Yaara used to live. This was the window through which she had watched me, and through which I'd first seen her.

I'd been submerged in the routine of those long, sorrowful August days, sitting awkward and bored in the wheelchair, there on the balcony across the way, while Yaara waved broadly at me, like those tourists on white ships floating gaily along mundane shores.

But soon, Grandma Miriam pulled my chair back into the dim living room and drew the balcony shutters with a racket. In the faint light that filtered through the cracks, she would lean in, eyes glimmering, and say, "Forget about her. Her father is a lousy Don Juan."

The next day, Saturday, after Zohara breathlessly gave me the news, I came across the test stick with its positive result. She had left it in a clear jar, like a prize, on the bedside table.

That evening, when two couples came to visit us, we all sat around the table in the yard, sipping beer, while Zohara made the announcement, proudly showing them the test.

As she shared with the girls that she believed she was already in her tenth week of pregnancy, and the others joined in with jokes about diapers, waking to a baby's cries, and how our lives would change in eight months' time, my mind started to wander. Amid that warmth, rather than recall my rural childhood, when my father was still alive, and my mother was strong at his side—I suddenly yearned for my dreadful adolescence. And at that moment, without understanding why, I began to brush the dust off your name, Yaara.

On Monday morning, I was able to leave the surveying office early and return to the same address alone. The old man opened the door and growled, his brows raised. He glanced behind him, then turned back to me and asked if I'd left my measuring tape. He looked again at the floor behind him. It glowed in the dusky light emanating from the wide-open balcony doors.

I gave him the short version of the story about my grandmother's apartment across the way, her surprising death, and said nostalgia had driven me to search for the people who used to live in his apartment before him.

We retreated to the living room, and he offered me a cup of tea. His feet were clad in thick, cast-like socks and orthopedic slippers. As he hunched away from me, he dragged them along, the soles rubbing against the floor like the exhales of a lazy train engine.

I settled on the sofa and rested my arm along the backrest, assuming I would now have a few minutes alone. My body sank into the soft seat, but I quickly sat up, restless. I rubbed my stubble—it was too long— and let my eyes sail around the living room. My gaze swept over a long, dark wooden bookcase stacked with countless books, their gilt lettering and titles weathered and cracked with the passage of time. Behind me, on the wall, hung two small oil paintings in matching frames, each a reproduction from Claude Monet's

Haystack series. Each painting captured a different moment in time, depicting the unique play of sunlight on the same landscape.

Perhaps I had time to sneak over to the window in Yaara's room? I wondered what that pale child in his wheelchair across the way had looked like through her window and whether the grayish-green shutters were still resentfully drawn on his balcony. But I couldn't muster the courage to stand, and instead turned the idea over in my mind—over and over—until I heard the clinking of a spoon inside a mug. My gaze was pulled through the door, toward a dim corner at the far end of the apartment, where the dragging of shoes was now growing louder. The silhouette of the old man emerged, carrying a steaming glass mug of brown tea in each hand.

"Right, right," he said, as though he hadn't left the room. "I don't own the apartment, and I'm having a hard time remembering the name of the owners now. My wife, may she rest in peace, paid the rent in advance. She used to be responsible for our finances. I'm a man of letters." His light eyes veiled over as he scoured his memory. He placed one steaming cup on the table with a tap, holding onto the other with his trembling hand as he slowly and carefully took a seat.

I sipped the dark tea and swallowed with effort due to the heat and sweetness.

My host puckered his lips to blow on his tea, then gripped the glass with two hands as he took a noisy slurp. We sat, wordless, for a long time, breaking the silence only with the sounds of sipping, breathing, and tapping.

"Let's step outside for a cigarette," he finally said. "Some air might refresh my memory…"

I got up to follow him. I don't smoke, but I was glad to leave the overly sweetened-tea behind.

"Go on, open the screen," he instructed, waiting with his back hunched, still holding onto the handle of the hot mug. He was watching me with parental patience until I managed to locate and unbolt a pair of locks.

He took a seat on a squeaky folding chair while I sat on the edge of the balcony wall. The old man placed his mug on the ground beside him. He dug his hand into the side pocket of his cardigan and rummaged until he found what he was looking for. He lit a cigarette, then leaned slowly forward to drop the scorched match into a turret-shaped basalt ashtray beside me on the wall. He then held out the packet, offering me one.

I shook my head. "No, thank you." It occurred to me that if this old man helped me track down Yaara, I'd buy him a nice lighter in return. I've always wanted to own a fine, metallic lighter, despite never being drawn to the habit.

"I like you," the old man said, taking a long pull on his cigarette and examining me. "Most of you folks are far less tender these days." He blew out smoke from the corner of his mouth, his face ponderous, a hint of sadness descending upon his formidable profile. He appeared lonesome as he stared at the darkening sky and at the treetops scratching the sides of the building, stirring beneath us like storm clouds.

"The family fell apart after the youngest son was killed," he said suddenly. "I had thought this apartment was their only source of income," he lowered his eyes to the floor and added offhandedly, "but later, my wife told me differently."

As he took a long pull on what was left of his cigarette, I nodded encouragingly, urging him on to the part about Yaara.

He stubbed out the cigarette before continuing. "Last year, when we were about to sign the lease renewal, the owner came with her daughter, an impressive young woman, and another man about your age, well-dressed. He acted like they were both his protégés. He was a serious brute with Tony Tucker shoulders who pinned the title 'doctor' to the start of his name when he introduced himself…" The old man closed his eyes for a moment, then rethought his previous statement. "Come to think of it, he was older than you."

In the silence that followed, I felt the envy caused by his words digging tunnels through me and stood up. But the old man, who paid no attention to my turmoil, and was spared the intrusive images assaulting my mind, was reaching for his mug of now-tepid tea. I could feel his eyes on me as I paced to the edge of the balcony.

Oversized white undershirts waved on his clothesline, along with thick men's trousers and a pair of pink young women's panties. Had I craned my neck a little further and glanced left over the wall, I would see the corner of my grandmother's balcony, but my attention was caught in a tangle of foreign contemplations.

"That," he remarked, "belongs to my caretaker."

I turned to face his scorched voice and found him hovering just inches away from me. I worried he'd caught me staring.

"Some of her clothes got mixed with mine," he said, his voice surprisingly unabashed. "She took good care of my wife, but I…I don't need anyone by my side." His tone sounded earnest, yet the statement ended in self-defense, his face flushing over, red and purple capillaries weaving through the skin on the tip of his nose and over his cheekbones. After a brief pause, I felt a warm, heavy hand taking hold of my shoulder. This was his way of signaling to me to come back inside.

"But if the people in the immigration department knew I wasn't needy, they would have her banished right back to where she came from. So, I let her stay. We have an arrangement." We crossed the threshold back inside. "So, now I find a sock here, a pair of pink underwear there. Everything she owns is pink… a pink wardrobe." He coughed, then added in a throaty whisper, "I don't like admitting it—" he wiped spittle from the corners of his lips, "—but you can tell she's letting loose. She spends all night out in town. Take a look." He widened his eyes and gestured with his broad chin toward the dark part of the apartment. "She must be sleeping in her bed right now. Just like a little doll. Stick-straight hair, brown from head to toe…" He blushed again.

"What did your wife tell you?" I asked by the door, afraid he was going to rest his heavy palm on me again to show me out.

"We've been renters here for five years, and thanks to the initiative of my son, who paid a handsome amount, the place will soon be mine." His eyes inflamed, his gaze sharpened.

I nodded.

He carried on, "Anyway, the owners lived here before us. The… Grossbars? No, Grossbards. They moved out seven years ago, maybe a little more. My wife said that after what happened, they barely made it through another year. The father of the family left shortly after the tragedy. And to this day, there's a locked room in the apartment, arranged with all the son's belongings." He counted on his fingers: "Posters on the walls, the bed made, a desk, and a closet with a boy's folded clothes." He cleared his throat and moistened his lips, once more wiping the spittle that accumulated in the corners of his mouth.

"Do you think we didn't complain? We did. She ignored it. Finally, she met us halfway and suggested lowering the rent just as long as we kept out of that room. The childhood bedr—" A coughing fit cut off his words, stemming from the hoarse breathing, thickening rapidly to suffocate him. His eyes seemed to demand an explanation for his coughing from me, but I could offer nothing.

Once he'd settled down, he cleared his throat again and said breathlessly, "I don't remember the details." He waved his hand cumbersomely, shaking his head as if hoping to shake off all thoughts.

I lowered my eyes with embarrassment, concerned I may have burdened him. Apologetically, I told him I had to be getting home and edged closer to the front door.

"My wife, may she rest in peace… she took care of everything. She also kept immaculate records." The old man promised to climb up to his crawl space in the near future and bring down a folder containing the lease. "And you," he said, wagging his finger at me, "can trust that the owner's address will be in there, too. I'm hosting a Bridge game here tomorrow, so come by the day after that."

I thanked him and left the apartment. The time I'd spent in the old man's company had been lengthy and thick. A pink darkness had fallen over the city, and people paced so energetically among the streetlamps that I cast another curious look at the sidewalk across the way, checking to make sure I could slip among them, and filter into that dynamic flow of pedestrians. I regretted not having asked if the old man could let me into the locked room, where time had stood still, leaving a frozen patch of the past in which we could wander. Internally, I was already visiting it, fearful of forcing upon it the present time.

I cannot remember Yaara's brother's name, and feel odd conjuring from the misty past that neglected-looking child who remains immobile in my memory; to charge him with the acknowledgment of maturity and death.

The scrawny young boy holding an apple walked behind Yaara in the procession that followed the gurney, carrying me out of the ambulance. It turned out that it was her brother. As soon as I was fished out of the back, the sun blinding me, my mother dawdling behind, Yaara ran alongside, peppering me with questions, which I ignored. As we turned onto the narrow bridge, one of the medics—a thick-set, heavily breathing man—pushed her aside. I was concerned the girl might have tripped or gotten trampled, but then, a little way ahead, up popped a head of glistening, flowing brown hair. I tilted my face sideways, and from the heights of the swaying gurney, I managed to spot her galloping on doe legs to the end of the bridge, where she waited beside the entrance, in the shadow of a wall covered with green ivy.

Yaara's brother stood in the building lobby, gaping at me with bewildered eyes. He froze in place for a moment at the sight of my bruised face and the crude metallic appendage affixing my femur, then fled fearfully, trying to beat us up the steps. The force of our upward trajectory pushed his bony shoulders against the railing, where he paused as I hovered in the tilted gurney above his small head covered in sweat-sticky hair, the same color as the partially eaten apple he was gripping in his small hands.

That is how he remains in my memory: holding an apple so big in comparison to his hands that it was like a basketball in an adult's grip, almost like a second head. The apple spread its sour-sweet aroma through the stairwell and was surely too much for the boy's appetite, having been tasted only sporadically, the gnawed parts oxidizing and growing darker in the interim.

Yaara's brother was about six years old at the time, and to think he'd grown and was killed… killed how?

I startled awake at night, mumbling my distress. I'd dreamt I was driving a hovering car that had suddenly plummeted into the abyss of an archeological dig site, zooming down its layers until its tires finally hit the ground. Then the rubble rumbled, and pillars of stone began to collapse, one by one, shattering and raising thick dust on the sides of the car, inside which I was trapped. Occasionally, a pillar crashed against it with a terrible clanging of tin. I wanted to cry for help, but whenever I opened my mouth, my teeth chattered uncontrollably.

I took a sick day without telling Zohara. Pacing down Oliphant Street, I recalled how—during the hours my mother spent resting in what had been her childhood bedroom, or hosting friends who came for a condolence visit—Grandma would take me and my wheelchair for a walk. With effort, she would push me up the steep, twisting alley and into the grocery store on the boulevard. On our return, Grandma would grip the chair's push handles tightly, her soft flesh trembling beneath her arm, as her biceps swelled, tensed to slow the rolling of my chair down the slope. I would sit with the grocery bag rustling on my lap, feeling the evening wind blowing in my face, agitating the tall bushes and the bowing stems of oxalis on the sides of the alleyway.

It almost always seemed to me that she was only able to turn the chair right onto the bridge at the very last moment, after which the wheels rolled smoothly and calmly along the paving stones. That was when the rattling of metal, which sent its continuous currents into the leather seat, died down, along with my aches and pains.

At this late morning hour, the half-flight of stairs was ensconced in thick shadow. To its left, beyond the wall and the gradated railings, my eyes were drawn down another short flight of stairs toward a sunbathed courtyard. That's where Yaara came from when she visited me, and now I descended it myself.

In the doorway, I paused to take a breath before continuing outside, glancing up briefly at the blue sky. I followed a graded granulite path that cut diagonally through a neglected yard, overgrown with hunched weeds, until I reached the shade at the entrance to the neighboring building.

When I arrived on the third floor and knocked on the old man's door, it opened only as much as the chain allowed. Through the crack, the face of a tiny Asian woman glared at me, her hands fastening her pink robe. The old man's name slipped my mind. I had trouble deciphering the handwriting on the sticker adhered to the bell and found myself facing the woman helplessly.

'Gur, from the surveyor's office,' I tried by way of introduction. 'He's expecting me…'

Her black eyes, the tight smile on her cherry lips—they deterred me. But when I saw her shaking her pretty head over and over again through the crack in the door, I got the impression they had indeed been expecting me. She suddenly turned to walk away, and I watched her through the crack, her vigorous barefooted steps and the silhouette of her robe against her thighs. Before she left my line of sight, she walked around an upright wooden ladder. The top nearly touched the hallway ceiling, much lower than the foyer ceiling. Crawl space doors on the strip of wall underneath it gaped into a dark maw of concrete and dust.

The shards of a whispering battle fought somewhere in the back of the apartment reached my ears like a broken echo: "You rest! He go now. Must want to steal. And you… you almost killed yourself because of him."

At the edge of my field of vision, a broken-up cardboard folder was gathered into a dusty plastic bag. That was the folder, I thought, and it contained the address. But the racket of the argument between the old man and the questionable young woman, still rustling through the apartment, already told me what to expect. I would either make it to the folder on my own, getting into whatever trouble I was going to get into, or I would wait helplessly behind the cracked door.

I slipped my hand over the chain, felt the edge of it, and ran my finger through its track. I closed the door hard against my forearm, and blindly yanked and rattled the end of the chain repeatedly, to no avail. The folder remained far away, casting a dull shadow on the floor tiles where it lay at an odd angle, wrapped in its murky plastic bag with the handles poking up like rabbit ears. If only I had a long hook at my disposal.

Minutes later, as I descended the stairs, the image of the woman's smooth skin and dark eyes that watched me through the crack appeared before me, followed, as if entirely separately, by the ugly twisting of her accusing mouth and words spewed in broken English and a lilting voice.

I was sorry for the old man who had fallen off the ladder and injured himself because of me. I felt banished as I walked down the asphalt path among the buildings, believing I would never show my face around this place ever again.

Over dinner, I informed Zahra that I would need to meet with Shahar in Herzliya's industrial area for some measurement work tomorrow. After some moments of doubt and concern on her part, she offered me the use of our Peugeot for my journey. This morning, as I left her at her office, she reminded me about our evening appointment with the gynecologist. I reassured her that I would be back in time to accompany her.

At approximately 1 p.m., Shahar and I completed the measurement of a rusting hangar at the vehicle service station. Following our formal exchange of hand waves through the windows of our cars, I made time to stop by and collect the envelope that Zohara had been reminding me about since the beginning of the month: financial support provided to me nearly every month by my mother, Zvia, and her husband, Elisha Bergner—an attorney and successful PR man who had shown no interest in his role as stepfather throughout the fifteen years of their marriage. Their apartment was in Ra'anana, and the envelope, as usual, was waiting on the kitchen island. I folded it, shoved it into my pants' pocket, then pulled on the doorknob to leave.

And there, in the slim gap between the marble floor of the apartment and the worn tiles of the stairwell, was a memory of Yaara, and the first time she had come to visit me in town.

Many years before the renovation, when the apartment was still modest-looking but the door was framed with the same brown metal as now, a girl with a shaved head stood on this line between the stairwell and the apartment. She was immersed in the murky gold glow of diagonal sunbeams that sliced through the marble every morning. Before I could even look into her dark eyes, my gaze fled from her bashful smile toward her feet, which stepped on our floors, bare and tan.

Now, in the elevator that gurgled down to the bottom of the shaft, I recalled the boy I used to be, and the melancholy of the time-paused body that had walked over the city pavers alongside that girl's bare feet. Across from the reflections offered by store windows, she told me about her agricultural school, about other boys who carjacked tractors in the middle of the night and jumped into fish ponds. Around noon, the sidewalk grew scorching, and Yaara hopped from one shaded spot to the next as I hurried after her, until we found cool shelter in a Ben & Jerry's shop. I paid for our ice creams with a note, dropping the change into the pocket of my black jeans, while Yaara walked slowly in her shorts along the black floor tiles, toward the back of the shop. I joined her at the round table she'd selected in a dim corner across from a mirror. She licked a purple scoop while I ate ice cream with a spoon from a Styrofoam cone.

—

The elevator landing on the ground floor snatched away my reveries. As I crossed the lobby, I noticed, as I always did, the large Cubist landscape painting by Albert Gleizes—it always evoked a sense of empathy within me for the solitary figure in a brown suit, climbing the canvas yet uncertain if he would ever feel a sense of belonging there.

I felt a powerful urge to take hold of something tangible from my past. My hands balled into fists, and

I dug my nails into my palms nervously until I exited the building. Then I remembered our family's photo albums. All at once, I could see a photograph from my youth behind my eyes, featuring you, Yaara.

I turned, stopped the front door from slamming shut, and strode back up the stairs to the third floor in the meager light. My energy depleted. I huffed as I pressed the elevator button to make the rest of the ascent. The button responded with a rhythmic blink. Was it possible that, just as we sometimes mistake an old photograph for a memory, I was now envisioning a blurry recollection as a photograph? I considered this with an uncertainty that weakened my resolve.

I stepped into the elevator. A tiny fan buzzed above my head. I pressed the button marked 7, and in the yellow light shone back my own reflection.

The naked nape of Yaara's neck, under her shorn hair, was so delicate and taunting. I had been secretly upset with her for chopping off her hair and was simultaneously ashamed of my stubbornness in refusing to accept change. I recalled her raising her foot onto the step of the bus, turning away before she walked upstairs, a tattered and faded lilac tote bag hanging off her shoulder. Three or four other passengers got on after her, the door shut with a puff, and I remained alone in the blue darkness, watching the bus pull away, its illuminated windows gaining distance.

I shoved my hands into the pockets of my jeans and watched my white basketball shoes walking measuredly down the sidewalk and pausing at the crosswalk. I felt weak and detached. I craved something that wasn't benevolent from Yaara, but at the sight of her tan, boyish shoulders, and elongated waist, which turned as she reached a hand to take hold of the bus rail, I was lost.

For many days, the bus stop on Ahuza Street, across from the department store, became inexorably connected in my mind with Yaara. Whenever I happened to pass by, her image would float before me: swimming and splashing in the fish pond with the boys, smiling wildly, far among the broad fields with their rustling green wheat and the whispering eucalyptus trees on the edge of the Youth Village at dusk, where the boys were barefoot and virile, skipping down the hot asphalt and pacing straight-backed along whitened concrete paths.

Through the elongated window, I watched the elevator climb up before it came to a halt. A tension in my shoulders must have signified a subconscious memory of the photo albums as I ascended because as soon as I walked into my mother's apartment again, I recalled their fate and bit my lip.

I could see the turmoil that had overtaken my mother as she bent over a wide-open album, her furious hands peeling and ripping its innards apart on each page, repeating the same act on all four family albums. Her hair spilled over her face, crisscrossing the fragments with shadow, and she reminded me of an agitated stranger blurring the boundaries of time and shuffling the sequence of our lives.

In spite of myself, I looked around for that floral cardboard box with gold metal along the edges, and as I did, a softer conjecture occurred to me: my mother was acting out of wild hope. I knew that state of mind well; it was the motive for the many brash changes she'd effected in our lives.

I continued to rush around the bright marble floor of the apartment in a frantic search until I reached the dim area at the end of the hallway and opened the door to my childhood bedroom—long ago converted into a home office. From the balcony, the boy I used to be glanced toward a neighboring building and spotted a tan woman sunbathing in the nude. When the woman caught his eyes, he thought she furrowed her brow with anger, but she remained lying on her lounger in the sun while he fled out of sight to his bed, heart fluttering.

Now, there wasn't even a bed in the room. A heavy wooden desk stood under the window. To its right was the narrow balcony door, and on the opposite wall was a bookcase made of thick wooden shelves, laden with a cluster of overstuffed cardboard folders, daily filing binders, and my mother's sheet music collection—among which stood an antique mechanical wooden metronome, set beside a collection of gilded deity figurines that disgusted me so much I had to avert my eyes. Had the box of photographs been there, it would have stood out to me among those symbols of tasteless spirituality.

Below the bookcase were three waist-high doors, locked and without knobs. The key poked out of one of the locks, its head round and its neck pipe-like. A half-turn and the lock clicked. The door opened an inch, and a rustle drifted out. Nothing of concern, until I sensed the growing pressure of spilling contents against the door. I quickly wriggled my free hand through the opening and pushed back a thick folder, from on top of which a tower of files was threatening to topple. Then I pulled my hand back and shut the door.

To open the other doors, I had to pull out the sole key and jiggle it through their keyholes. I was prepared for an avalanche and twice was relieved when it didn't happen. I knelt between the open doors and rummaged through the compartments.

The floral box I found in the left compartment was lighter in color than I'd remembered. A stack of home videos that no one would watch again leaned against it. I carried the box from the dimness of the sideboard and down the dark hallway, clutching it with both hands, heading for the living room, where a diagonal sunbeam filtered through long shutters.

A shadow of former guilt had me fretting that I might accidentally knock the hammered pecan bowl from the living-room table; I knelt carefully and placed the box on the sun-spotted rug instead. I stirred the contents of the box, flipping through countless pictures of my mother, developed in saturated Kodak print, which filled the first thick stack of photos. Most images of my mother were taken on vacations and outings with different romantic partners. Always wealthy men who liked to take her picture. Perhaps it was because of how tall she was and the cumbersomeness of her long limbs—which she treated as an embarrassing flaw. Or perhaps it was because of her slight buck teeth, which left a faint bite mark on her handsome bottom lip, and which to this day ignite bouts of bitterness toward her parents, who never got them fixed. Or perhaps it was the yearning of a woman who had become a widow at such a young age. At any rate, it was a barely visible hint of aspersion that twinkled out to men of a certain type.

I could picture the long line of suitors who visited our home throughout my adolescence, and could conjure up each of their personalities, in search of the essence of said aspersion, but I found myself too uncomfortable to do so. So, for now, a quick glance at this mighty pile of colorful photos, which hindered my path to the images I was seeking, was sufficient to satiate my memory.

Finally, I picked out photos that I'd set aside and gathered the others, which I'd scattered over the rug, spilling them back into the box and closing the lid.

I sat down in the armchair, holding the three photographs like a fan in my hand. I would have leaned back and looked at them more closely if I hadn't experienced an unpleasant tingling up my left leg. It had been bent under me as I sat on the rug and had fallen asleep, and yet I still jumped up from the chair and anxiously shook my leg around, as if trying to scatter an ant swarm.

Fears for my body and guilt toward my mother for burdening her with my pain are tangled within me. In my pacing, I crossed and recrossed the sunbeams, which now broke into flickers along the rug, ripping and repairing the strings that fastened the outside to the inside.

The guilt weighed on me, but from the moment I returned the floral box to the sideboard and walked out of my mother's home, stepping from the shadow of the building to the scorching sidewalk, I felt a growing sense of relief. Had I let my legs lead me, they might have taken me to the corner, where I could look longingly to the west, toward the bus stop outside of the department store. But now, with three photographs in my pocket, a tempting and incriminating loot, I aimed my gaze higher, considering a return visit to the old man to try and gain access to that file once more.

I looked around for a nearby, semi-isolated spot where I could study the pictures before returning to my car and the rest of my life. A side street lay to my left, the parallel boulevard. I stepped off the sidewalk into the parking lot of a neighboring apartment building.

It was eleven o'clock, and a few cars shaded the hot asphalt. I wondered if the sunbathing woman still lived on the penthouse floor. Many years had gone by, but an odd sensation ran through my limbs, along with my adolescent fantasies about her. At night, she appeared to me in my dreams, attractive and vindictive; every day, as I walked to and from school, I feared I might run into her.

I made my way to the tangle of brush at the edge of the lot, tense-bodied and gripped by the feeling of strange eyes watching me, until I came across a broken curb. I ducked among wild bushes and entered a tiny patch of wilderness, cast in damp shadow-light—one of those dwindling hideouts that my heart was always drawn to whenever I walked through the city.

At the edge of the tangle, I bumped into a thick root, and my feet faltered down a crumbling slope. A branch scratched my arm, and I landed on the sidewalk at the bottom of the slope like someone kicked right out of a brawl.

I found my footing and whipped my head around. Across the narrow road, a loud group of boys were gathered around a bench in the shadow of boulevard trees. I preferred to get some distance from them before crossing the street. A block or so down, I sat hesitantly on a bench, from which I watched the boys for a few seconds longer before pulling the photos out of my pocket. I placed them on my lap, warm and somewhat curved. I was in no rush to turn them over. First, I had to feel relaxed. The place and time certainly fit the bill: light foot traffic, the faint sounds of cars on distant, busier streets humming around me with cradling regularity. Every so often, a gust of wind rustled through the treetops, ruffling the embroidery of their shadows on the pavement at my feet. I watched as the shadow patched itself up again in countless natural and convincing patterns.

I turned over the single picture of Yaara—the most recent I had left of her. Someone had taken a picture of us together during my only visit to the Nahalal Agricultural Youth Village, where she boarded during the term. I recalled how the photograph had reached me through the mail several months later, during a winter twilight. Yaara had written her name on the envelope in round letters. I took it into my bedroom, where I opened it and found inside a piece of folded white paper containing the photograph.

The three of us had our arms around each other: Dror Kaplan in the center, arms open, leaning against our shoulders in a generous embrace full of youthful confidence. His round head juts forward, the beads of his eyes looking directly into the camera. To his right, Yaara is wearing a faded lilac T-shirt with the neckline cut off, draped loosely over her tan body. Her flowing hair swells over her forehead, and her round eyes look out from under the shadows of her lashes, their gaze secretive. My right arm leans hesitantly on Dror's back, my head tilting away from the other two, watching them from the side, remote and lost. Even now, I can feel my reservations about Dror at the tips of my fingers, and the revulsion that touched his bare shoulder inspired me. An artificial camaraderie.

An outside observer would not have guessed that I'd only known Dror for two hours—two hours I had longed to spend in the company of Yaara, during which I found myself accompanying them in their wandering through the Village. I remembered his last name because other boys we ran into along the concrete path and near the farm sheds called him Kaplan, while Yaara referred to him as "Drori" in the frivolous conversations they conducted about routine affairs—the kind that seduces a foreign ear while also defying it by leaving out details, using local slang, and sharing inside jokes. A dog, a chiseled boxer, who ran alongside us, occasionally stepped away to sniff around the shaded yards before huffing back to the head of our line. Dror and Yaara watched its tense muscles twitching and discussed lockjaw.

"We used to have this old neighbor," Yaara said. "I would walk her dog after school. A little terrier she treated like her baby. One morning, when she took him to visit some relatives in the village, an aggressive boxer lunged out of a yard and attacked her little dog. She told me that the poor guy surrendered right away—you know, flipped over on his back, legs up in the air. But the boxer locked his jaws around him and tore him to bits." Yaara swallowed. Behind her serious expression, a puzzling hint of laughter bloomed, the way it does for those who struggle to process their mourning.

Dror tried to grill her for more details, but Yaara ignored him, enveloping herself in silence, as if regretting her cold phrasing.

A feminine gasp tore me from my memories. Right in front of my bench, close enough to touch, a young woman grabbed onto her partner.

"What's wrong?" the man asked, his voice calm. He was as firm and sturdy as a laundry machine, and the words he spoke came out distinctly, placed one on top of the other like bricks in a wall.

"Nothing, I, I just…" the young woman giggled awkwardly, shooting me a quick look.

As they drew away from me, he held her closer, and she slipped her hand into his back pocket. She thought I was a homeless person. And, for a moment, I felt as if I was. Perhaps I envied them. But what for?

I couldn't blame the woman. I'd left home this morning in my work clothes as if it were another day of field measurements—a ratty T-shirt and blue cargo pants with holes and rust stains. I ran a hand over my sprouting beard, startled by its length. Zohara would complain later. She seemed so far away all of a sudden. She knew nothing of my frantic search, and I could not share my disappointment and glumness with her.

My resolve did not weaken, but I was concerned that, in my current state, the other photographs might inspire unbearable sorrow. I stood up and shoved them into my front pocket. The photo of myself as a child in the company of my father was committed to memory anyway. I'd often memorized it. It was just that today, when I found it among the sea of pictures, I wanted it all to myself.

—

At home, I plopped down on the bed, arms spread on the sheet above my head, my heavy shoes sticking off the end of the mattress. My head was full, and a thick fatigue spread through my limbs until I could no longer lift a finger. A remnant of red light, brightening over my closed lids, blackened. The duskiness tightened inside me, and finally, an echoing dark void blocked the pathways into my consciousness. Any effort to conjure the photograph from the Youth Village and expand the array of memories connected to it was bound to fail.

The dark, boundless space spun around me for long moments before little pulls of light began flashing here and there, like slits in paper. From within them ran out the muscular boxer, rushing away from me, fading into darkness only to reemerge elsewhere, propelling himself with the force of his twisting back, his tail pointing out between the muscles of his buttocks and his hind legs, which flew through the air. The proud male rushed through my mind once more before becoming lost in the pitch black, inside which echoed the voices of Yaara and Dror, chatting about lockjaw. They described a tragedy, and she lowered her eyes as if embarrassed by my presence at her side as she spoke so crudely.

—

I startled awake. In the meager evening light, I saw Zohara's silhouette crouching over the bed, shrouded in a black shawl.

But it was just the chair, a pile of clothes heaped up on the back. My heart was pounding. I sat up on the edge of the bed, debating whether I'd been awakened by the silhouette or the terrors of the dream. I was burdened by the impression that a foreign force had breached my world. I mumbled, "I must hurry to get her," recalling the OBGYN appointment we had at seven o'clock, and I dragged myself to the shower.

As I shaved, watching the sink fill with stubble, the face that looked back at me from the mirror seemed childish, and I felt miserable. Even two additional scars uncovered by the razor did not hinder the impression of the child's petrified terror beaming from my eyes.

I wiped the remains of the shaving cream from my face and swallowed down an anti-epilepsy pill to stave off the seizures that had been plaguing me ever since the accident. I turned off the lamp and undressed in the dim bathroom. In the narrow shower, I leaned my forearms against the wall and closed my eyes. The harsh stream lashed at my hunched back for a long time, while my nine-year-old self dropped his own clothes on the floor and joined his father in the shower. As the man threw his head back under the hot water, plowing his fingers through his wet hair, my childish eyes followed the path of the soapy water as it rolled swiftly down his tan body, dripping from his genitals to the floor through tassels of wet hair.

His masculine body, which had made quite an impression on me as a child, associated itself troublingly with his burial. In my imagination, my father was lying naked in the dirt, and clumps were tossed over him with a sickening thunk. The vision tormented me for many nights before its details finally blurred, leaving me enslaved to its seductive horror.

I sat up among the covers, hesitating before opening my eyes to the empty darkness. The echo of marching boots still pounded in my ears, resembling the heartbeat of the fetus I had observed on the ultrasound last night. As these echoes gradually faded into the quiet of our bedroom, I was reminded of the terror that had gripped me as I fled them in my dream, seeking refuge within the entrance of a dim, broad hall. There, nine high, narrow windows projected a painfully blinding sunshine. Iron hospital beds were arranged in perfect rows, and in each one, a baby wailed, swaddled as tight as a cocoon. I scampered among them, frantic, until, a great distance away, an empty bed winked at me. But the closer I moved to it, the shorter it became.

Zohara was deeply asleep to my left. Her naked skin, white and smooth, gleamed brighter in the darkroom than the glowing hands of the alarm clock, which stared piercingly at me from her bedside table.

The coolness sharpened. I felt around on the floor for my shirt and put it on. I walked over to my pants, draped on the back of a chair, and pulled the photographs from the pocket. For another long moment, I watched Zohara lying on her back with one leg bent, and then left the room.

Her pregnancy folder was on the coffee table in the living room. Last night at the café, she had smoothed out the ultrasound pictures on the table between us with excited fingers and proceeded to talk nonstop about the images and the baby's pulse. I eyed them suspiciously while she emphatically pointed out a human fetus in the amorphous spots—either because she was supposed to or because she had so wanted proof of her pregnancy that was more tangible and rewarding than morning sickness.

In the light of the candle on the café table, the faint, twinkling caramel and honey color in her eyes reminded me of the three tones of the freckles that glimmered in the sunlight over the bridge of Yaara's nose. Her high cheekbones and the graceful flutter of her lashes came to life in my memory, gradually captivating me, while Zohara gushed on and on.

Now, I turned on the standing lamp and sat down on the couch. I carefully examined Yaara's face in the photo from the Youth Village. Her delicate freckles had evaded the camera's lens, and her portrait, contained within my mind—painfully palpable but absent from my real life—worsened my longing for her.

I stood up all at once, and a shudder ran through my shoulders. Like a defeated poker player, I dropped the photographs face-up on the table and moved to the wide window, from which night peeked out through narrow cracks between the shutters. I brought my face closer to the chilly pane, and fear rose in my throat. The battalions of thorns that had been gathering around our house had grown numerous under cover of darkness ever since the evening when I'd circled the yard with my father-in-law. He had rebuked me for my lack of maintenance, but I had done nothing since, and now it was too late. The thickened weeds had gained power and were branching tall before my eyes.

My body was gripped in delusion. Almost involuntarily, I began to rub my fingertips against my forehead. They had hardened like rakes. Gradually, the rhythmic squeaking emanating from my skin to my ears began soothing me. My fingers loosened, and my eyelids found respite in the warmth of my palms. My father appeared before my eyes, barebacked, raising a scythe in a thorn field, his sweaty shoulders glistening in the burning sun.

—

Later, in the early hours of the morning, when I looked at the photograph again, I built a small wall in my mind that separated Yaara from that solid man who called himself "Doctor." The triangle of mother-daughter-man also contained another option, and the more I thought about it, the more the old man's remarks about the age of the man came to mind—how he had taken back his words, correcting himself by saying, "Come to think of it, he was older than you."

Due to my health condition at the time, I was transferred by ambulance for a short drive from Hadassah Hospital in Jerusalem to Noga and Eldad's home in the village of Beit-Zayit. Noga was a peculiar sculptor, and he was my father's half-brother—a tattered, taciturn man who ran a farm in the village.

I'm not sure how long we were supposed to stay there, but a sight I remember well is of my mother spending countless hours gathered in an ochre corduroy armchair in the dimly lit corner of the living room or pacing restlessly around the house. Eventually, it became clear to her that she needed to be close to her mother. Years later, my mother told me that this abrupt change in her plans gradually strained her relationships with Noga and Eldad. This was mainly because Noga—whom my mother described as less mentally stable than Eldad but more controlling—interpreted my mother's actions as a lack of appreciation for their efforts to help us, leading to years of resentment.

Among all those fading and secondary memories that I can easily recall, and just as easily bury, the saddest one I have, from the evening I arrived at that rural house in Beit-Zayit, is still the most prominent...

Feeble and pale, I was pushed in a wheelchair from the front entrance out to the driveway, the ambulance having departed mere moments before. An outdoor lamp shed meek light on the wide façade of the house, and a warm breeze blew out into the yard—merely a clearing in a thick forest. A rustling of leaves sounded from within the foreign darkness that hovered between the dense trees.

Eldad and another man I didn't recognize approached me with a hose where I sat in the wheelchair. I looked around frantically for my mother, but as they began to wash me down, I realized she wasn't coming. There was no choice, no possibility that I could be carried up the narrow, twisting stairs that led to the bathroom on the second floor. I surrendered my battered body to them.

The water poured over my fresh wounds, taking on the brownish-yellow hue of antiseptic ointment, pooling on the leather seat around my thighs and spilling down to the concrete below. When I was drenched and shivering with cold, one of the men pulled me up by my shoulder, supporting me from behind even after I'd managed to find some steadiness on my right leg. Eldad, if I recall correctly, was the one who dropped the hose to the floor and knelt down. He pulled a towel from his shoulder and dried my thin body with careful, distant motions. He helped me put on some light clothing and then used the same towel to dry the seat of the wheelchair.

As they guided me slowly and cautiously back to the seat, inducing pain in every movement, Mom stepped out of the shadows, tired and silent. She thanked the men softly and leaned down toward me. When she placed a tender hand on my bony shoulder and looked into my eyes, I recognized a dampness in hers. If she spoke at all, they were but a few words, forming slowly out of empathy and distress.

"Do you need anything?" Eldad asked her softly.

She shook her head, no, but when she tried to push my chair, Eldad bent down quickly to unlock the brakes for her. Then he remained standing on the wet concrete, damp towel in hand, watching as she pushed me back toward the black front door. From the narrow foyer, she rolled me guardedly into a side room and closed the door behind us.

A jar-shaped lamp cast orange rings of light on the wood paneling. A narrow, mussed bed stood against the opposite wall, and above it, a small window overlooked the garage. My mother dragged a wooden chair and took a seat in front of me, beside my outstretched injured leg. She took a deep breath through her nose, then slowly, as if feeling her way through the dark, she took my pale hand in hers, looked at me with compassion, and gave me the news.

—

I have recreated that awful night many times and learned over the years that my severe injury left a scar not nearly as bitter and deep as that from the death of my father. It is odd that all I remember from the moment of the announcement is the setting—the bedroom, the orange glow—as well as the child I used to be bursting into tears and crying, "I knew it! I knew it!" helplessly, the sobbing breaking the barrier of my throat, stifling and painful.

—

"Do you want to tell him?"

Zohara liked to start conversations from the middle. When an idea had been bouncing around in her mind, she assumed it had been bouncing around in mine, too, and so the words that reached her tongue were often shorthand summaries that she wanted to confirm out loud. Only rarely did she have dilemmas that actually required my opinion. I frequently had trouble catching up to her train of thought, having spent many minutes justifying her beliefs in brief, not convinced about what I'd just given my support to, only so she could continue in her stride. In spite of my concern, Zohara had never, to this day, stopped to make sure I'd been truly listening, since she was always one step ahead. If she claimed I was on her side, it was only out of a sense of unity she'd imbued upon herself.

That warm evening, I was sitting on the edge of the bed, and Zohara was standing barefoot behind the closet door, looking at her body in the mirror.

"About such a big thing in your life," she added softly. Judging by the circular motion of her sharp elbow, I guessed she was still watching her own reflection rub her lower belly.

Her pregnancy was still barely noticeable.

Her mellifluous idea of sharing this "big thing" with my father repulsed me. It was infected with the same brainless optimism that steers romantic comedies,

New-Age ideas, and symbolic acts that believers like to refer to as "closure." And yet I acquiesced.

The ride over on Friday morning was pleasant enough. We chatted a lot, and by the end of the drive, there were two empty to-go cups of coffee between us.

—

A small military ceremony was being held outside the main entrance to the cemetery, blocking me from taking a right and parking in the familiar lot, from which I could pace hesitantly along the grimy asphalt, recreating my first visit here with my mother.

Almost a year had gone by since my father's death when I first passed, silent and deferent, through that heavy black iron gate, which was fixed in the gap between the thick trunks of a pair of dusty cypress trees. I still recall our footfalls against the gravel, that moment when we left the asphalt and tentatively approached the patch of land seeded with a meager row of tombstones and fresh mounds. The air was humid with shade and irrigation. My mother sat down quietly upon my father's tombstone, her back hunched. She lowered her eyes and rested a hand against the light marble. Her long fingers, like the fingers of a blind lover, caressed the outline of the engraved letters of my father's full name, then distractedly fluttered over the dates marking the thirty-six years of his life. A long line of ants crawled through the crack between the dirt and the stone. I heard my mother sniffing.

"It's… good to cry. Crying is a… release." Tears choked her voice. She sniffed again, sighed, and then gently wiped her eyes before looking at me, appearing a little surprised. Probably because, as she cried, I took a step back and leaned with my hands crossed behind my back against the trunk of one of the cypress trees.

A loud truck lumbered down the twisting road on the way to the kibbutz where my father grew up. The rattling of the motor intensified at the top of the climb to the cemetery, and as the truck moved away with a softening, stifled growl, a new silence fell over us.

Mom filled her lungs, her narrow shoulders rising. She looked up, and her eyes, which squinted when she cried, opened wide. Pointy treetops framed a peaceful blue sky. A few pearly cotton clouds hovered high above us, and the edges of the sky were brightened by sunlight.

"I want to believe," she said, trembling, "that Dad is watching us from above." She finished speaking with an emotional swallow.

At that moment, I noticed that I was fingering the bark vigorously while my mother's words continued to sound in my ears like a strange third voice.

In the first five years, my mother used to take me on an annual cemetery visit. I never cried at my father's grave, because whenever I was there, I felt stifled, as if my body was repressing the tears burning inside of me for the sake of protecting my frail mother. Even when the urge intensified, making me tremble all over, I felt strong enough to defeat it until it dried in my throat.

"Let's park there," Zohara pointed.

I continued slowly down the road alongside a low brush, between two flapping flags, where soldiers in pressed uniforms gathered with their backs to the cemetery, standing at ease in two short rows. While other soldiers, who seemed more senior than them, rushed around in the breathless activity of final preparations, they lazily donned berets at an angle on their shorn heads.

I turned right after the cemetery, as Zohara had instructed, into a large gravel patch, beyond which fields and orchards stretched out, and beyond those, the green hills that led all the way to the Golan Mountains on the horizon.

The ground crunched, and agitated stones creaked under my tires as I drove behind twelve other cars, which parked, one by one, against the flanking cypresses, until finally, I found a spot for our rusty Peugeot.

Zohara stepped out of the car, carrying the empty cups.

"Leave those," I said, slamming the door and moving around the front of the car.

Zohara sighed demonstratively and leaned back inside to return the cups to the back seat. My eyes wandered restlessly to the view of cowsheds among the greenery up the hill, imbuing me with a dark, unrealistic yearning for my father's younger days. Zohara leaned against the car door, her hands empty and her expression restrained.

Civilians came out of their cars in groups of twos and threes. A mother and father. A mother and a girlfriend. All looked as if they'd come to see their loved ones in the military ceremony. Some of them must have never been here before and never would have been, if it weren't for the ceremony. Their presence bothered me. I knew that if I'd come here without Zohara, I would have turned the car around, and returned the way I'd come, feeling banished. At that moment, as we crossed the parking lot, I certainly was not expecting the turmoil this visit would cause in me.

We walked into the cemetery through the back entrance, but rather than following the path that leads past the monument of a roaring lion—the memorial the others were all here to pay tribute to—and on to the military plot, I pulled Zohara aside. Like infiltrators, we walked over a rustling bed of dry cypress needles on the northern outskirts of the cemetery, among the lines of trees and tombstones blackening with age, until we turned by a tree on the corner.

I lowered my eyes as we walked, facing the sun that flickered over the treetops in the south. Beyond the gray trunks to our right, soldiers still stood to attention. As we came nearer, shreds of ceremonious speech emitted from a mobile loudspeaker system reached my ears, like an echo reverberating from the surrounding hills.

We were almost at the end of the asphalt path, just about to descend the moderate slope toward my father's grave, when a pale memory of another grave was resuscitated in my mind. I pulled Zohara aside toward the depth of the cemetery. There, among thick bushes and lonesome tombstones, we uncovered a lost path from my childhood days.

My father's sister had died of cancer at the age of seventeen, and my feet led me to the tombstone made of basalt rocks that her siblings had made for her. On one of them, they'd engraved their sister's name, as well as the dates of her birth and death: March 11, 1952, to April 13, 1969. On another, they'd copied, in a thin, screeching scratch, the verses of a poem she had written mere weeks before her passing. Profound sadness and care had been invested in these rocks, placed upon a burial plot arranged like a tiny rock garden surrounded by rich, wild vegetation. I stared at it for a long moment, struggling to connect this labor of love with the five dull-hearted individuals who cut us off completely after Dad died—his parents and three siblings.

I felt Zohara's hand fluttering over my stooped neck.

"Did your father ever talk about her?"

I shook my head and cleared my throat. We were silent for a while longer until we turned back toward the trees.

The sun burned over the treetops, its rays blurring in the dust below the waists of the cypresses. In the distance, I saw the path descending toward my father's grave, and the changes made to its surroundings seemed so crude and foreign to the character of the place that it felt like a nightmare. A concrete path glimmered in the August light, newly cast on the route to my father's grave. It had been set a few centimeters off the ground, with no space to set foot in the gap between the concrete and the tombstone.

Wordlessly, I paused on the path, alongside graves lined like boats beside a dock. The place I'd once known had been taken away from me, and in the seconds that passed, even Dad's tombstone seemed to draw further away, lost in the mist, while only a cluster of coal-black letters continued to flicker before my eyes.

Zohara stood silently beside me, sharing the width of the path, glancing at my face from time to time. She gently offered to give me some space and shifted around me. The movement of her body against my back made me restless. Then, the tapping of her shoes against the concrete shot my nerves once and for all. I was enraged about the difference this little path had made, and childish tears filled my throat. Just then, on the backdrop of all that, Zohara's heels tapped in a broken, restrained rhythm—attesting to the fact that she was moving slowly, hesitantly away. Yes, I knew this side of her personality. She wanted wholeheartedly to be "good," but her unripe heart and her orderly mind were no match for the spasms of my soul.

I broke into bitter tears.

Only on my way back did I manage to get a hold of myself and wipe my eyes. I promised myself that I'd return to visit the grave on a gray winter day, when the light would be fainter.

You didn't want to tell him?" Zohara asked. She was waiting, straight-backed, alongside our gray Peugeot, waving her long arms at the cemetery as if my father were standing by the rear entrance, on the backdrop of the roaring lion, awaiting my news.

I shook my head and ducked into the car.

Zohara drove silently down the twisting road. When we got to the intersection, she stopped, turned to face me, and asked, "Want to talk?"

"No, I'm fine. Let's stop for coffee soon."

"I don't know. I feel more like being in nature." She sped up and merged into traffic after a military truck that entered the highway from the direction of Metula.

"All right," I said, even though, when I was in a dire mood, I feared nature. Everything within it seemed to contain danger.

"Are you mad at me?" she asked after a while.

"No. Are you mad at me?"

"Me? No. But you're acting weird."

"I don't know. I guess… I guess I'm disappointed these things still get to me."

"The path?"

"That too."

"And?"

I stared at the dense dust my shoes left on the floor of the car. I could feel Zohara on my skin, turning her eyes briefly away from the road to look at me.

"Hard to say," I finally admitted.

"Is it because you didn't tell him?" she replied.

"It isn't about that."

"You went there especially to do that, and then…" she encouraged. She was speaking slowly, gauging the effect of her words on me, her tone growing more hesitant.

We left the car in the scorching sun and walked into the thicket. Zohara found a twisting route for us up a gradient incline flanked by pine trees. We walked toward the misty light of a clearing. She slowed down to walk beside me, a thin blanket folded under her arm.

Examining my face from the side, she said, "I still think you'll be glad you did it." Her voice sounded odd in the swarming silence.

I looked at her, puzzled. For a moment, I didn't follow her meaning before I connected the dots.

"Yeah, I don't know. It's just that my memories of him mean more to me than some gravesite."

"It's your father's grave. It's got to mean something."

"I didn't say it doesn't mean something. It's just…" I slowed down even more. Zohara matched her pace to mine.

"Going there really affected you," she said, looking at me tenderly. "You're tearing up."

"It's just that people attribute so much importance to graves and tombstones, but those are some of the few symbols in life that people can't choose for themselves."

Zohara sighed. Our silence wore on, and I could tell I sounded avoidant to her.

We found a yellowing grassy knoll, its edges layered with pine needles. Zohara, who was afraid of snakes, trod carefully and alertly as she peered around for a patch clear of any thorns and rocks where she could spread the blanket. A dull yearning ran through me. I dawdled as Zohara examined the ground.

A short while before my father's death, I had gone camping with him. We woke up late at night to watch Halley's Comet shooting through the black skies with its bluish tail. I'd asked when we could see it again.

"The comet?" Dad said, then explained in his typical calm tone, "In another... seventy-three years."

I widened my eyes at him.

In the same tone of voice, he added, "You'll be eighty-four, and I'll be... I probably won't be alive anymore."

A short while later, we had returned to our extinguished bonfire, the dirt underneath it still damp with our urine. Dad zipped himself into his sleeping bag. Shortly after, I could tell by the sound of his breathing that he'd fallen back asleep, but I still tossed and turned for a long while, a dark and hollow horror having crawled into my heart, as terrifyingly empty as the sky we'd been standing beneath. I had no words with which to explain it to myself beyond a vague acknowledgment of the fleeting nature of life.

Just a few months after this, a truck crashed into our car as we were driving down the curving road from Masada National Park to Jerusalem. Our Subaru flipped over several times, eventually coming to a stop upside down in a jagged ditch. Like rolling dice, we each were destined to a different fate. My father was killed on the spot, while I eventually made it out alive.

"Come here, my sad man. I know the ultrasound stressed you out. But look at my belly. You can picture it, can't you? A tiny little baby, the size of a peanut?" Zohara was becoming emotional, looking at the gap between her finger and her thumb as if she saw something in it I could not.

When I didn't offer a sufficient response, she lay down on the blanket she'd finally spread over the grass.

I wandered along with my thoughts for a while longer under the trees that flanked the golden lawn Zohara had picked out. When I came closer, a small, mysterious smile pulled on her lips. She searched my face until her mischievous eyes found mine. Then she lifted her shirt over her ribs as if she were alone, threw her delicate neck back, and blinked her golden-lashed eyes at the sun, which filtered through the canopy above our heads. The silhouettes of leaves fell upon the whiteness of her skin, distorted but as clear as shadow play.

She looked so out of place in nature, with her pure paleness. Three beauty marks shaped like drops of chocolate drew my eyes in, and my gaze skipped up from the one on her belly to her ribs and then higher.

Then I lay down on my side next to her. Zohara looked at me askance, placed her hands on her waist, and then slid them down until the tips of her spread fingers met at the bottom of her stomach, emphasizing the modest bump. She had a shallow, oval belly button with a small skin tag curled inside of it, like a stunningly seductive bud. But that tumultuous day, it inspired a hollow worry within me. Before I could decipher it, Zohara pulled the hand I'd been using to support my head, and I collapsed onto her chest.

She giggled. Her hand was on the back of my neck, and she pulled my lips to her stomach. I wriggled free, got to my knees, and stormed her bare feet with kisses. Zohara's laughter died down as she swallowed softly, then fell silent, filling the air with breaths that grew more and more submissive.

I'd never given her feet this much attention, or any other woman's feet, for that matter. But now Zohara was moaning underneath me, spreading her arms along her body and arching her back. The moaning was Zohara's, but the feet—oh, those feet at the end of the blanket, writhing like a pair of fish in my hands—were tan and chiseled. I bombarded them with kisses, using my fingers and my dampening mouth to wipe away the dust from the Village paths and the dirt of the fields that Yaara had trodden.

Innocent Zohara, how much pleasure she'd experienced. In truth, we were both overtaken by it, surrendering to the heat of the precious moment, so much so that I had no idea whether any curious onlookers had passed us by.

For many days, I was haunted by a delusion from the cemetery, in which I saw my father's tombstone swept into the sunny maw of a blinding future. Most of the time, the vision hovered over me like a semi-translucent demon, imbuing me with a hollow distress. But in lonesome moments, the distress would exacerbate, burdening my mind with its full weight.

Zohara was watching a game show, filling the small living room with excited voices and flickers from the screen. I walked out to the backyard, slamming the door behind me and instantly regretting it. The thorns out back only added to my disquiet, so I walked around the house to the front yard. In the grainy darkness, lit only by a faint street lamp, I recalled Meir Israelis, the therapist who had treated me when I was an architecture student and still felt a passion for creation. He was a lonely old man with kind eyes and a forehead plowed with horizontal wrinkles. When he was listening, he used to nod his head and twist his face. When I said nothing, he said nothing. He spoke little but was determined to help me. I was stubborn, and so therapy was as useful to me as windshield wipers in a storm: as long as they're operative and you keep your hands tight around the steering wheel, you make it through somehow.

I felt differently about him after he died. A decade or more had gone by, and I didn't prioritize attending the funeral; I had work that seemed more pressing. But I went to the memorial service a month later, at a civilian cemetery, and was dismayed to find a group of men and women gathered around a gray tombstone atop a small mound of healthy weeds. They settled into place while whispering and then spent a long while indulging in their uniqueness: reading letters to the deceased, shedding tears, or simply shooting the others looks that seemed to say, *I'm different. I'm not like you. After all, I was his close friend. I was like a child to him.*

In the two years that had passed since, my attitude toward him had softened, and from time to time, I had conversations with him in my head. Now, I imagined he would have claimed that the concrete path at the cemetery recalled the feeling of being abandoned. The first abandonment, Meir Israelis would have explained, was obviously the death of your father, the reverberations of which continue to ripple all around you. Now, twenty years later, they simply hit you again, harder, in the presence of your wife, on the path among the cypress trees.

But I recoiled at the interpretation I had planted in his mouth because I remembered that, on that hot day, when the shadow of my body fell at an angle upon the tombstone, along with the stifled anger igniting in my mind, my muscles tensed as well. The more I pictured the work of casting the path—performed, I imagined, by cold-hearted laborers—a kind of familiar tingling, more than unpleasant, ran through my crotch, signifying my humiliation. One of the humiliations I'd imagined my father experiencing in moments of helplessness had now found a peculiar outlet in my body.

First came the visions of his burial, which haunted the nights of my youth. Another one formulated in my mind fifteen years ago, when, proud and emotional, my mother described her boyfriend Elisha watering the plants by my father's grave with devotion, using a long rubber hose borrowed from the cemetery custodian. And now it was the concrete path.

Anger, which had been stifled, now bubbled up, spreading like an ink stain, reaching out its arms. There were people behind these actions. They were an articulation of the time that barred me from my father. By the force of those crude souls that pulled the plows of the present, I once again saw those cold-hearted men in blue work coveralls casting the path between nailed planks, as if obstructing my journey into my past.

Blue graph paper was waiting for me on the desk in my office. On a yellow Post-it note, scratched with his angular handwriting, Shahar demanded I complete the blueprint as soon as possible because it had been due last week, and the client was getting nervous. If that wasn't bad enough, by 9:30, Shahar was already standing behind my chair, breathing down my neck.

In moments like these, I tended to sense the distress of the architect I thought myself to be when facing such a mind-numbingly boring task. But, that morning, I saw the blueprint as a call to voyage. I was missing the measurements of the room with the locked door, but I possessed the length of the hallway and the width of the neighboring room—Yaara's room. Using those, I easily extrapolated the size of the missing room in the blueprint. Shahar had been right at the time: there was no point in inconveniencing the poor old man. That was how he phrased it, his tone respectful, using words like "poor" and "inconvenience" only minutes after he'd almost broken the door down with his knocking.

Had Shahar insisted that the locked room be opened, the old man, with express reluctance, would have shuffled away into one of the other rooms, where he would have opened and closed drawers, rummaging here and there, finally returning from the dimness with measured steps, a key pinched between his fingers. Would I have realized at that point that I was looking at the bedroom of a dead boy? *Killed,* the old man had said. In our country, words like *died* and *killed* differentiate very different kinds of demise—*killed* being the superior of the two.

"Was he the owner? The man we met?" I asked, feigning innocence.

"The old man?" Shahar snorted. "That scatterbrained guy? He'll be moving to assisted living soon, and his son will be renovating the apartment."

"His son?"

"Yeah, the owner of the bodega downstairs. I buy my morning coffee from him." Shahar yawned and took a quick, loud sip from the black coffee in his Styrofoam cup. It was as if he were having his picture taken for an ad. "And my dad buys a lottery ticket from him every Thursday," he added. He tipped the remaining contents of the cup into his mouth, showing off swollen deltoids and biceps that puffed up the fabric of his short-sleeved shirt.

I went back to sketching. Shahar lingered beside me, saying, "He's already added a warning in the land registry form, and the current landlord let him run the measurements. She realized he was in a rush to renovate and then gain a profit by selling on the asset." He nodded knowingly, sipped his coffee, and sighed with satisfaction.

I looked up over my computer screen. The coat stand by the front door, made of curly black bamboo shoots, looked too homey for my taste, exacerbating my overwhelming sense of being out of place. Shahar's ironed shirt was hanging on the hook closest to the door. To its left, like a skinned animal's fur, was his father Simeon's itchy-looking sweater. I'd heard him talking on the phone for a long time, on the other side of the wall, and could see him, in my mind's eye, pacing his office like an animal in a slaughterhouse, naked of his fur and abundant with jiggling flesh—a horrid image I kept pushing out of my mind as I worked.

Shahar left, leaving the Styrofoam cup on my desk, containing the sediment of his coffee and a grainy, muddy trail. The hanging shirt was part of the unrefined atmosphere, while I sat there, looking official in my button-down.

I had trouble giving up on the idea that the old man would be the one to deliver Yaara's address to me. I felt a growing intimacy with him and suspected that some lie had been fabricated to get him out of the apartment.

The son was nothing like his father. The bodega he owned on the corner was a bizarre cross between a kiosk, coffee shop, and tiny casino. His body was full and composed of ovals: his face was round, his belly sturdy, and his eyes flashed with the schemes of a hedonist. I could easily picture him stripped down to the waist, barbecuing, whispering hunks of beef on a grill at a park, or drinking in a club downtown, surrounded by his posse while a stripper rubbed his thick thighs and kissed his bald head. And yet, something about the general impression he relayed did connect him to his father.

I watched him for a few moments while pretending to browse. He was staring at a TV that hung over the window overlooking Paris Square, occasionally rearranging the snack shelf or digging and stirring the nut and seed tubs with a metal ladle. He swayed around with boredom that also contained anticipation for the arrival of the perfect customer—someone who would spend a fortune on lottery tickets or cigarettes.

A pack of cigarettes of the brand my employers smoked winked at me from the display, sporadically appearing from behind his curved back as he moved. On the shelf below it, I saw packs of *Time* cigarettes, such as the old man smoked. I bought one, tore off the plastic wrapper, pulled out a pristine cigarette, and stuffed the pack along with the plastic into the pocket of my jeans.

"Got a light?" I asked the owner, my voice full, waving the cigarette at him.

"Seven shekels for the lighter," he replied, turning away from me and busying himself with something I couldn't see. "If you want to smoke, you have to step outside."

"Can I bother you with a few questions?"

"No, I'm working," he asserted, not turning around.

I decided to forgo a semi-clear orange lighter and made my way inside—the cigarette, a foreign object pinched between my fingers, pointing at the stained floor. A doorway from the bodega led down three steps into a narrow room. Before descending, I turned back to the round-faced owner and ordered a coffee, hoping that, when it was served, I'd have another opportunity to start a conversation. I had to speak up and repeat my order twice before he even noticed me. Then he nodded his heavy head and reached a hand to the coffeemaker.

In the meantime, I took the steps down, crossed the room, curving my body around closely arranged tables and chairs, and took a seat at the back of the room, where there was a little more space. I placed the cigarette on the table. It was faux-wood Formica with black metal legs, bringing to mind an elementary school teacher's desk.

The room was a windowless gambling hall where an exhausted air conditioner hissed, and a TV screen hanging from the low ceiling showed game scores and raffle draws. On two opposite corners, two men hunched over gambling forms, scratching or filling out numbers vigorously, like occupational therapy patients chasing an impossible dream.

The owner took the stairs down with a heavy step, balancing a stainless-steel tray upon which trembled a glass mug of steaming coffee, a spoon, and a porcelain bowl containing sugar packets. He approached my table, hugged his thick fingers around the mug, and served it with a wide twist of his body, his elbow passing before my eyes. Then he stood straight, gripping the empty tray. I intended to capture his attention before he removed his host's cloak and assumed he wouldn't do so before I took my first sip. I raised the mug slowly, pausing as I held it against my lips. Then I looked up, a question ready at my throat, when my host surprised me by asking, "No sweetener?" His tone was severe, scolding.

"What? Sugar? No thanks."

"I can't live without it. And look where I ended up."

He snorted, looked around, and added with excitement, "Living among chocolate, candy, and bonbons." He licked his upper lip distractedly and returned to the front of the store once again.

I sipped on my coffee, embarrassed. The beverage burned my mouth. I forced myself to swallow it, and it lit up my organs, as one-dimensional as boiling water. This seemingly meaningless bodily event caused the timeline along which I traveled to thicken with happenings, and it felt longer than its true course of five seconds. When I looked up, the round man's face seemed higher and farther away.

A pair of customers arrived, standing in front of the nut display on the edge of the busy street, blazed in sunlight, chatting with the owner. I envied the customers for conducting such easygoing chitchat with him, as he folded and lined up brown bags laden with snacks into an orange plastic bag. Finally, he tied the bag loosely and handed it over with that same wide motion he'd used to serve me the coffee. When they left, I got up.

The owner glanced behind him and spotted me walking out to meet him. He turned to look at me. This time, he blinked those oval eyes, either in order to adjust to the dimness or because he'd been caught off guard. He seemed to have forgotten all about me in the last few minutes, and now I was returning, blurry, into his awareness.

"That's it?" He jutted out his chin.

After I'd already left, but before I crossed the street at Herzl Hair Salon, I turned around and went back to the bodega, where I waited pointedly beside the counter while the owner spoke on the phone. He said a few words and then submitted to silence, listening to the flow of words on the other end. He furrowed his brow, his face gradually taking on the appearance of a struggling student.

But I, in a stubbornness unnatural to me, held his wandering gaze until he gave in, removed his fat palm from his sweaty forehead, raised his brows, and signaled for me to stick around.

When he hung up the phone, I looked straight at him and repeated my question, this time mentioning Yaara's name, which hadn't met my lips in years: "Can I bother you with a few questions about Yaara Grossbard?"

The man slammed the drawer of the cash register shut and looked up, interested.

My voice grew occasionally hoarse as I told him about myself. At the edge of my words, when I gathered my courage and asked for his help in tracking down a lost childhood acquaintance, the man's face continued to express attentiveness, but his eyes rose above the lottery tickets on the glass counter and drew toward pedestrian traffic. A shadow of doubt moved across my heart. I'd known my share of disappointments. I wondered if the trust I had in him was a result of nothing more than his blue eyes, which reminded me so much of his old father's. My spirits were low. I was watching the loose skin under his chin when, all of a sudden, he returned his attention to me and started to speak.

First, he informed me that apartment eight in the building on Laurence Oliphant Street was owned by Ms. Dalia Nahum Grossbard, a mother and a divorcee.

He'd only ever seen the face of her ex-husband, Yigal Grossbard, in a faded copy of his identification card. At meetings, his place was always filled by his proxy— a young attorney.

"Shlomi Manoach, the man whose wife you're looking for, owns a jeep auto shop and a rescue and towing company. His business is called *Field Doctor*. He's a strong, stubborn man who conducts real estate negotiations for his mother-in-law. He attends all meetings with lawyers, but he isn't a party to the agreements. That's why his information doesn't appear on the contract. But his phone number…" The man reached for a small notepad, then thought better of it and said, "Just call the auto shop and ask for Shlomi. That's what I did."

He shoved a thick snack into his mouth, chewed on it, and crumpled the wrapper in his hand. At this stage, as he shook his head with pleasure at the taste, I gave up on the idea that he might offer any further help. I was prepared to leave him like that, with a drop of caramel glued to his lower lip that still twitched with satisfaction.

"Hang on," he suddenly muttered between munching sounds. He raised a finger, swallowed, and said, "The girl. She was the one you were asking about, right?"

"Yes," I breathed.

He tossed the empty wrapper into the trashcan and ran a tongue over his gums. He told me that they'd held a semi-formal meeting at the apartment before closing, the purpose of which was to secure a guarantee from the current owner that the locked room would be cleared out. Here, his voice faltered, and he tapped his fingers for a long time, their tips staining the glass counter with murky grease. He sighed and started talking again, filling me in on all the tragic details I already knew. When he was finished, he hung his head, swaying between agitation and empathy.

"When we were renters, it was a different story," he suddenly barked. "We were considerate. But now that we're buying the place—it's absurd, isn't it?"

He was so upset that I nodded my agreement, adding a flaccid, "Yes," and feeling like a traitor.

"Well," he took a deep breath and sighed, "it's behind us now. But that time, the landlord brought her daughter to the meeting. The two of them wanted to say goodbye to the place, and I could tell it was emotional for them, so I offered to make everyone coffee. I remember that Shlomi takes it black, no sugar. He tugged on his skinny pants, sat down on the couch, and watched us like some kind of emperor. In the meantime, the mother and daughter walked around the rooms, holding each other. The daughter..." He shook his head slowly, as if watching shards of a painful recollection.

"Listen, I felt sorry for her when they came back to the living room. We were all sitting and talking, having coffee, and the mother put her head on the daughter's shoulder and cried, as if it hadn't been years. I'm not criticizing, God forbid. Eventually, they sat down on the couch across from me, and Yaara said she would be in charge of clearing out the locked room. She asked her husband if he would help, and he said, 'Yep,' like a hammer blow. Gradually, Dalia pulled herself together, wiped her tears, asked us to excuse her, and went to the bathroom to wash her face.

"I complimented the daughter on how supportive she was being. I was being genuine. But she was modest. You know? She had a modest smile. After that, we had to coordinate when exactly they would come by to empty the room. She told me she'd been working as a nurse at Carmel Hospital for the past three years. She walks to the hospital every day, passing through the avenue that's across from the street where the apartment is, but never finds the courage to turn. Then she said nothing, stared at the open shutters, and whispered, 'It's been a long time, and it isn't easy for me, either, just like Mom.' I remember her exact words because her whisper sent shivers down my spine. It was like we were alone in the room."

—

Some time went by, and the rectangular bulge of the cigarette pack remained in my pocket. I'd have to get rid of it. I pushed the thought aside, because the whisper that had sent shivers down the bodega owner's spine now seemed to be breathing into my ear, as fresh and new as the moment when Yaara's whispering lips came together and pulled apart with the slightest dripping sound, the tip of her tongue clicking delicately against the roof of her mouth.

"Like we were alone in the room," he'd said. I could hear the thrill in his voice.

———

I set my stakeout spot on the terrace of the café on the corner of HaNassi Boulevard—Yaara's daily route from hospital to home. I ordered a small latte, and, carrying the warm mug in my hand, used my hip to open the door, which screeched against the uneven floor. From the sunny side of the terrace, an albino woman in a wide-brimmed straw hat, with hair that flowed down her bare shoulders, looked up at me. Apart from this woman, who crossed her legs in a gesture of ownership, the other five tables were unoccupied. I ambled over to the shaded side and took a seat at the farthest table I could find.

As I sipped my coffee, I angled my eyes over my mug and watched the woman perusing a tattered yellow booklet, as thin as a notepad, which she held in her long fingers, her nails bitten down to the quick. I took another sip and used the pull of the warmth and bitterness in my mouth to focus my mind on the task at hand. Before I even swallowed, I decided to turn my back on the woman. I watched from behind the terrace railing, my eyes trained at the edge of Bikkurim Street, into which several other smaller streets flowed, some of which I thought may have served as shortcuts.

But perhaps today, of all days, Yaara was tempted to come in contact with the memories lurking in the hidden slope of Oliphant Street. There, in the shade of whispering pines, on the path curving moderately between low stone walls, I could hear her footsteps louder than the bustle of the city. Aware of her lonesomeness, I could see her looking at the entrance to the building with awe and yearning. Her feet knew the narrow bridge, the descent down the worn steps to the yard trapped between buildings. But with every step she took, sorrow intensified within her. So she only peeked through the savage tangle of thorns infringing on the path leading to the dark lobby of the building where her childhood had been cut short, then retreated up the steps and lengthened her stride along the path.

I let my imagination run wild, because now Yaara was striding up the curving alley, and her shoes—a nurse's Birkenstocks, most likely—would soon tread upon the shabby asphalt of Bikkurim Street, which she would walk up—until she saw me.

Yet only a hunchbacked old man swayed heavily up the steep pavement, along the hedge. From time to time, a car weaved a familiar strand of noise in the tapestry of the city ruckus, and the old man would look up longingly, then lower his face to his shoes again after the car had passed. By the time the man completed his toilsome voyage to the street corner and took a break, I gave up. In truth, my head was full even before that time of grumbles against my cowardice, which dissuaded me from looking for Yaara at the hospital. I was coming up empty here at the café, and my alertness was fading.

In the meantime, the albino woman removed her hat and shook her neck until her hair hung over the back of her chair. Her golden eyelids fluttering, she let her tender skin indulge in the lukewarm sunbeams of the end of the day. I was familiar with this kind of restrained attitude toward the sun. Zohara's hair was also as fair and lackluster as a doll's, and through her body, I became familiar with the pearly pallor of melanin-deficient skin and the pinkness concealed between its folds. Perhaps because of those, when I was in the presence of this woman at the café, my conscience consumed me. When she left, I felt abandoned.

I downed the rest of my coffee and walked out onto the sidewalk. I spotted the woman's fair head and locked my eyes around it as it drew away from me down the moderate slope of Ahuza Street—still without the straw hat, surrounded by darker heads and growing dim in the twilight. The sight of her head affixed in my memory as a kind of negative of a different memory—perhaps the sight of Yaara's head with its flowing pecan-hued hair as I witnessed it from the gurney on that scorching afternoon twenty years ago. I continued following the pale spot that grew blurry and lost among the human tangle, until I could no longer tell if I was seeing it with my eyes or with my imagination, and so I turned the other way.

I crossed the street at a diagonal and fell straight into the plaza outside of the Cinémathèque, where pairs and small groups crowded the ticket booths and stood on the sidelines, talking. Like a bubbling porridge, their voices congealed in my ears into a seductive yet repulsive exhibition of relaxation that was so foreign to my state of mind during the minutes that had taken me here.

Finally, I found shelter among the greenery at the public park. This is where, in similar twilight hours, Grandma Miriam used to take me for some refuge from the stifling apartment. When we arrived, she would park me by the bushes on the line between the asphalt and the lawn, at the heart of the garden, duck down to lock my chair's wheels, one by one, and then stand back up, often letting out a soft moan of discomfort that concealed an embarrassment before turning away from me.

Though in all our visits, my grandmother made sure to position me with my back to her, meaning that

I was facing the lawn where children played, I could still picture her sitting, coiled up on the bench by the hedge, her alert amber eyes bouncing watchfully between the entrance to the garden and the faces of passersby. I was familiar with those tense expressions her face wore under such circumstances, as well as her heavy cheeks, underneath which a small, stiff jaw shifted.

It was this way, as well as by force of pinches or painful squeezes, that articulated a peculiar affection— she forced a secret life and an aggressive estrangement upon herself, while simultaneously warning me against intimacy.

Now, I strolled over to the edge of the lawn. Behind my back, on that same dark bench across the path, a homeless man was bundled up in rags. The wind carried the sweet scent of pine trees from the shadows, rustling in the crown of weeds that surrounded the blue memorial pool, while the water pouring loudly into it reminded me of the tumult of the masses of which I'd been so wary.

On odd days, my grandmother worked at the Mashbir department store as a cosmetics sales clerk. When she returned home in the early afternoon, she'd linger her eyes on the picture of my grandfather Rubi, who looked at her peacefully with his button-down shirt from the wall by the door. Then, she would wander around the kitchen, where she always found tasks she viewed as urgent. Only afterward would she go to the bedroom, kick off her heels, lie down on her side on the bedspread, and leaf through a women's magazine, distractedly wiggling her swollen, burgundy-painted toes, which peeked out of the edges of her tailored slacks.

Once, she broke her habit: on entering the apartment, she invited me to go out with her. When I agreed, she shoved a magazine into a glistening leather bag hanging from her shoulder. After making all the necessary arrangements, she rolled me in my wheelchair over to Manya Park, parked me on the lawn, and locked the brakes. She stood beside me for about a minute in quiet restlessness, then went to the bench, leaving me in a cloud of familiar perfume—at times fresh and at others sour; the smell of another's body, the kind that filled the bathroom in her apartment, thickening the sense of estrangement I felt there (my foreign body looking back at me from a foreign mirror).

At the edge of the garden, to my right, two rowdy boys kicked a ball around, approaching the lawn right in front of me. I guessed all this from the way they called out to each other and the growing sound of the ball against the soles of their shoes, as I didn't turn to look. Finally, the ball hit the armrest of my chair. I glanced around, startled, and saw it landing and rolling off along the lawn, while a shirtless boy chased it. His friend, who had stayed behind, followed him, calling out warnings, but not crossing the line of bushes that hid him from view. In the meantime, the boy returned with the ball, and the moment he kicked it in an arc toward his unseen friend, he spotted me for the first time.

I can't remember what he cried out in a grating voice before he looked away with a restrained smile, but from the distance of years, I still recall a malicious spark in his eyes and the heat of the blush that took over my face. I looked down to the wheel on my right, where a short shadow melded my body and the wheelchair into a distorted shape.

I spent long minutes sitting across from the barren lawn, my heart curled up inside me, until finally, I heard a yelping bark approaching. From among the thick bushes flanking the entrance to the garden, Yaara emerged, pulling behind her a frisky, sand-colored terrier. Her shiny legs in shorts cinched at the hips, and her pair of shabby braids swinging as she walked attracted my eyes. A long moment went by before Yaara turned toward the lawn and finally met my gaze.

For a thrilling fraction, it appeared that our bodies wanted to meet, but the presence of my grandmother raised a wall of awkwardness between us. Yaara walked onto the shimmering grass, knelt down, unleashed the dog, and from the moment she tossed a stick for the pooch to chase, her entire mischievous being was aimed at me.

Darkness congealed in the depth of the garden, and now the delusion appeared before me inside of a halo that glowed like the moon. Within it, Yaara appeared to me, so tangible, just as I'd seen her that day, confirming my gaze within hers, her dimples foretelling her intention.

My point of view was low in the wheelchair as a soft hand ran over the back of my neck, as faint as a breath. Gradually, the footfalls of pedestrians passing through the garden dwindled, until, in a quiet moment, I imagined that adult Yaara was standing beside me, watching along with me as a puppy played with a girl with braided hair.

A thick branch was tossed, and the golden terrier galloped after it into the bushes. He stirred through the twigs and emerged with a bark. Empty-mouthed and fast-breathed, he ran over to Yaara. She called out, "Vachi! Vachi!" When she sprawled on her back in the grass, her T-shirt rode up to reveal her lower stomach. The dog pounced on her, and she curled her thighs and grabbed him with both hands. He licked her pretty face, and she stuck out her tongue and mimicked his motions.

In another part of my brain, I saw Zohara and the fetus curled up in her uterus. The two of them slowly constructed feelings of guilt over my abandonment, and this completely took over the charm of my longing. I stated my case to them, arguing that no action had yet been taken. But my heart palpitations and the shudder in my muscles, from my shoulders down to my palms, got the better of me, and I headed to the bus stop.

Though I hurried over, I arrived in time to see the rear of the bus loudly leave the curb, pulling a whirlwind of rusty smoke behind it, and I slowed down with acceptance. I stood with my back to the hedge that protected battalions of shadows behind it. So militaristic and alert it was that the breeze that blew in my face barely fluttered its leaves.

On the other side of the street, a tiny Asian woman in a pink skirt suit dragged a pink suitcase behind her. I waited for her to get ahead of me, then crossed the street and followed her. She pulled away from me with a vigorous step, just as I'd seen her do at the old man's apartment, through the crack between the door and the frame, turning her back on me and walking down the hall. Now, too, I felt her begrudging me, but I still followed her for an excessive amount of time, until she took the steps down into the Carmelit Underground station and was swallowed in darkness.

The vibration of the cold bus window against my forehead imbued my body with a cradling calm, broken sporadically by a rousing bang, a kind of malicious trick played on me by the driver. I looked hazily between the backrests. Only a few passengers remained on the bus, ensconced in the darkness that the highway brought upon us.

The engines roared an admonishment, shaking loose screws and sheets of tin. The noise died down, transforming into an introverted purr, as if struggling to forgive. My eyes began to close, and visions came to me through a trembling crack in my eyelids. I gave myself over to the simmering emptiness, until, behind my back, I heard a child whispering in a teasing lilt and turned around to find that an octopus of darkness had sent thick tentacles all the way to the back of the bus, through a dozen empty seats.

—

Back home, I felt I had forgotten something behind… I was laid out on my back, shrouded in a cast from head to toe. Yaara walked over in a nurse's uniform, holding a black, buzzing device. Rather than assist me, she lit a Time cigarette, puffed on it, then recounted her recollections:

"The phone rang all night long, people calling and calling. I remember how, at dawn, a quiet misery descended on all three of us. But only at sunrise did we realize the living-room windows were wide open. Mom, who had been pacing all night, plopped down on the couch and wouldn't move anymore. It was as if we'd accepted a piece of bitter reality. And then the military funeral, and…"

Yaara sighed morosely, blew a decisive plume of smoke, and wedged the cigarette into the corner of her mouth. She ducked down with a screeching circular saw and sliced long slits in my cast. Then she released my neck and my upper limbs from the white plaster with the help of crude metal tools.

Once free, I wriggled my arms and legs around with wonder, but Yaara didn't bat an eye, instead continuing her speech as if she were talking to herself:

"…and I was so embarrassed by the neighbors across the courtyard, who must have heard all about what had happened. To them, we were like three actors on a stage. In the corner of the living room was the dull orange light of the standing lamp with the white lampshade that filtered the beam. Dad sat, stooped, at the kitchen table. And I—there was a point when I got up from the couch and padded quietly into my brother's room, which looked foreign and unfamiliar in spite of all the everyday objects in it. I lay down slowly among his bedclothes, and that familiar smell, the smell of his body in the sheets…" Yaara took a long inhale through her nose, eyes closed, then whispered, "His smell melted the artificial strangeness in the air. And I fell asleep with my face in his blanket, maybe for ten minutes. Do you mind?" she asked, lighting a fresh cigarette, pinched between two fingers.

I was about to answer, but Yaara started the saw again, fixing her eyes on the rotating disc and increasing the speed until its buzzing made me shudder with fear. She noticed my apprehension, and a soft, sarcastic smile twitched at the corners of her mouth.

Then the saw was gone, and Yaara lit one cigarette off the butt of the other, took a puff, and murmured, "I started smoking at nursing school…"

Then she stood up, looking particularly tall. Her legs, clad in skin-colored pantyhose, drew away, and only then did I realize she'd been sitting on the edge of the sofa where I'd been lying. I wanted to get up and follow her, but I was still mummified from the waist down.

Unsettling implications concerning impotence and castration, which were presented in my reverie last night, weighed heavily upon my thoughts. As I rested my elbows on the office desk, I found my gaze hovering aimlessly amidst an array of architectural blueprints glowing on my computer screen.

In the passing hours, I found myself recollecting that Zohra's morning sickness confined her to our home today. And the delicate figure of her materialized as if from thin air, right here, amidst the quiet hum of the office's computer fan. Spreading her slick white limbs on our bed, waiting for me to return. Holding onto this image as a potential way to restore my sense of manhood, I somehow managed to focus on my work. Finally, at the eleventh hour, a door toward relief swung open for me. Shahar informed me that he was accompanying his father to a lunch meeting, and with a resounding slam, they vanished behind our office door. I listened carefully to the fading echoes of their conversation as they drifted down the corridor. Soon enough, I seized the opportunity and slinked out of the office.

—

By late afternoon, I was lost under the tranquil presence of summer's sky, enveloped in a soft, ethereal glow, taking the shortcut, meandering through a silvering olive grove, from the bus stop toward the backyard of our house.

As I neared, the disturbing sound of screaming engines became louder in my ears. From the shadows, peering through the thorny veil, I saw two men in front of our house, raising motorized shears and fervently breaching the tangle of thorns that rose to the height of their shoulders. Behind their backs, which were curved in healthy effort, and all the way to the path leading to the house, were trampled heaps of cut brambles. The dirt they exposed and trod upon with their heavy boots was strewn with the skeletons of truncated thistles and rumpled weeds.

I recognized our neighbor, a robust and stocky farmer with thick gray hair. But the one whose presence in our yard made me grit my teeth was his son, Yuval—a young stud with a healthy and disciplined physique who participated in all of his father's farming endeavors, and toward whom I'd developed a fickle combination of hatred and envy ever since we'd moved in. This was not due to any negative qualities of his but because, to me, he was the embodiment of a fate that had been snatched away from me when I had my accident, when I was uprooted from my childhood village.

"Zohara must have called them," I muttered as the sweat trickled down my face. I hurried through the yard, feeling the sting of thorns as I crushed them under my shoes, evading the men at work. I skirted behind the weathered shed, tracing the edge of the house until I reached the front door.

I found her in the living room, wearing boxer shorts and a T-shirt, no bra, leaning against the frame of the open glass doors and watching the yard. Our home was cast in shadow, and the yard was an illuminated continent of green. The rumbling of motors choked and broke in a sequence of screeching sputters. The men set their tools down on the ground. Our neighbor stretched and gulped some water from a plastic bottle, narrowing his eyes at the burning sun. The son, Yuval, pulled on the ends of his shirt and used it to wipe his sweaty face. Then he bent his tan arm and arched his fit back to pull some green stalks that had caught between his shoulder blades.

Without advancing, I watched him from the darkness over Zohara's shoulder. She stood in the doorway, her right leg reaching forward, fingering a vertical fold in the curtain. I watched her running her hands slowly down the crease and wondered if she missed me. Then she turned around, as if having heard a worrisome rustle.

"Oh, good, you're here." She smiled languidly, then added, feeling out my mood, "They said we're gonna surprise you—"

The end of her word was swallowed by a loud motor sputtering to life, choking, then starting up again, emitting clouds of thick smoke and the odor of burnt gasoline that carried on the wind through the open window.

"Why are they here?"

"Because of the snakes. I've told you a million times, I'm afraid they'll get in the house."

"Really? You don't think I could have sheared the bushes myself?"

"Relax, they're doing us a favor." Zohara lowered her voice and turned to look out at the yard again.

The neighbor advanced slowly across the wide yard, while Yuval, who seemed to be drawing power from Zohara's eyes, sheared even more vigorously, moving farther away, hewing a dark corridor through the grass. Seconds later, I turned to walk away, leaving Zohara to watch him. The door, made of heavy wood that had been covered with many layers of paint over

the years, was already turning on its axis, slamming
behind my back.

The sound of shear motors was like a pair of
enormous flies circling our yard, and as I drew farther
away, their racket evaporated into the air. But Zohara's
image—standing there, looking outside with great
curiosity while rubbing a fold in the curtain—was what
fixed itself in my mind.

I continued to ponder my jealousy and the
meaning of the mysterious, unaware smile that had
insinuated itself on Zohara's thin lips whenever we ran
into Yuval, who was always in a sweaty, crafty rush.

Two days later, at dusk, I took a seat on the
balcony of the café again. I sipped an espresso and
closed my eyes, still enchanted with Yaara's moments
of innocence. It was as though I was still there with her,
all those years ago—in the middle of a game of
dominos on the glass table, she pauses to count her
friends on her fingers and detail the nature of her
relationship with each and every one of them.

Your pretty face, the appearance of your pearly
white teeth, and the jealousy that contracts my heart.
On days when you don't come to see me, I look
through the shutters at the road, climbing up to the
street to see you walking home from school with your
friends. You are always with the same boys who tease,
shove, and snatch each other's backpacks.

But every Wednesday, I wait in the foyer, listening for the tapping of your sandals on the stairs and the whisper of your backpack strap as you slip it off your shoulder before knocking on the door. You come to see me in my bed while I am suffering from one of those inexplicable headaches. I awaken from troubled sleep to see you removing a cold compress from my forehead; my mother had applied it a short while earlier, and now you dip it in the bowl on the table. My eyes close heavily. I hear the water dripping as you wring out the cloth, the drips slowing down, growing farther apart, until, from within the darkness, comes the touch of your dainty fingers as you place the heavy cloth upon my forehead.

You remove your hand, and I turn your way. You whisper, "Sleep… I'll be your doctor now." My eyes close again. The next time I open them, I see you standing in the shadow-light on the other side of the glass table, then sit down on the rug and open a textbook.

The three photographs stuck to each other as if perspiring. I had to peel them apart, even though, only days earlier, I'd wrapped them in the folds of a yellow sheet of paper, as Yaara had done years ago to the photo of us she'd mailed me from the Youth Village.

Taking a large sip of yet another coffee, I returned the photograph of my father to the paper, along with the photo of Yaara, myself, and Dror. The other one, in which Yaara appeared by chance, lay in my palm. She was far in the background, and I hadn't even noticed her the day I'd grabbed the picture from the box at my mother's house—I had taken it simply because I intended to tear it to shreds: it reminded me of an awful period in my life.

But some indulgence of melancholy made me look at that photo again one night, taking another peek at the image of me lying, injured and pale, on the made sofa at my grandmother's apartment. That's when Yaara's face was revealed to me, in the distance, the way it had materialized the first time I'd seen it—and I understood why she had me spellbound.

Thanks to this photo, the entire room gradually appears in my mind, covered in old, grayish-brown wall-to-wall carpet. Like a mangy dog, the carpet was plagued with bald spots along a route worn from treading, highly visible at the entrance to the room, then blurring, and becoming prominent once again where it turned left, aimed at the balcony—overtaking a sitting area with a pair of couches and a light armchair, gathered around a rectangular dark glass coffee table full of reflections and hidden flickers, like a fish pond at night.

On the day the picture was taken, a tablecloth had been spread diagonally over that table, but the corner of the cloth closest to the sofa was folded in on itself. In its place, a brown pharmacist bottle containing hydrogen peroxide cast a deep reflection in the glass. Alongside it, several sterile pads were stacked with a bundle of sterile paper packages of cotton swabs as long as meat skewers. I remove the blanket from my body and cautiously lower my pants, unveiling my injured leg to Ira, the nurse who visits me once a week for check-ups. She approaches the sofa where I am lying, with my mother standing beside me.

"How is leg?" she asks in broken Hebrew, her voice professional and impersonal.

I nod, hearing the back of my neck rubbing against the pillow, as mother answers for me, "We're fine, aren't w—"

"I check," the nurse cuts her off, sharp and matter-of-fact. She rips open a paper bag and pulls out a pair of gloves, which she dons on her hands.

As my mother retreats from me, her blouse brushes against my face, carrying with it a familiar scent that invades my nostrils. It is the same one that lingers in the darkness of my parents' closet, in the perfumed depths of which I used to bury my head among the hanging clothes, sneaking forbidden glances at my father's reserve duty rifle.

The nurse takes my mother's place on that thick, virginal patch of carpet where the table usually stands. She bends to examine my left thigh, but as her gray, icy eyes linger on my wounds, I notice a worrisome alertness forming on her face.

"It… go down to the bone," she says, as her fingertips press tenderly around the sensitive edges of my wounds.

"What?" my mother asks, startled.

"These nails. They go all the way down to the bone, and if no sanitized…" the nurse says, taking a close look at those four moist, swollen wounds, each resembling the gaping crater of a volcano around a stainless-steel rod the girth of a knitting needle. She delicately touches the wounds again. Each time her fingers press against my skin, a faint groan escapes my lips, but it is quickly stifled by my awareness that my mother is watching me with concern from across the table. I close my eyes, preparing myself for what is to come. I hear the nurse tearing the sterile wrapping.

Abruptly, my breath catches as I feel the firm press of the hydrogen peroxide-dipped cotton swab against the damp wound near my hip bone. The pain doesn't come right away. Firstly, it is a burning sensation against the skin, which deepens and exacerbates as the substance invades my body, tracing its way down the narrow gap between the rod and the moist flesh, causing my muscles to tighten and tremble while I'm biting into my lip with increasing force.

The pain will not abate, and already, a second swab burns me at the same spot. The nurse works meticulously, and the more she treats my contaminated wounds, the more I suffer. Finally, I break down and cry as if I am haunted, shaking my head and resisting the nurse's repeated pleas. Desperately, I gaze up toward my mother, seeing her face contorted with sobs, causing me to choke back my own.

Sofia, my mother's childhood friend, comes inside from the balcony as I am crying, and the five guests who have been sitting out there with her all glance in my direction. Yaara is among them. Sofia walks over to my mother and hugs her fragile shoulders from behind, while I bite my lips, and the nurse continues to sanitize the rest of my wounds.

———

In the moments when my mother's sadness weighed heavy on my heart, almost without realizing I was doing it, I yearned for my father, or, at the very least, for a sibling to balance out the power dynamic between her and me. Once I became aware of this desire, I agonized over it, feeling that by my very wishes, I was pouring salt on some invisible wound in my mother's body.

As a child, I overheard my mother talking about how difficult it was for her to get pregnant, as well as describing two painful miscarriages. It was as if her body had fought tooth and nail against gestation, I thought, as I heard her arguing to her friends that her narrow hips were not meant for childbearing, or whenever I saw her undo her pants to show them the smirk-shaped scar from her C-section—a decisive response to their wondering why she didn't want to have any more children.

In searching for the garden furniture, I moved slowly along the side façade of our house, ducking on and off beneath the low branches of the lemon trees. Just as I got down on my knees and spotted a folding wooden table and two matching chairs leaning against the stony side of the house, Zohara's face emerged, haloed by the warm glow of the sunset from around the corner of the wall. Bulbous clumps of spider webs hung from the joints of the furniture, their legs drenched in moisture from the leaf-padded dirt, which reeked of citrus rot.

This neglected, worn-out garden furniture was infected with the morose essence of this home, one of any number of objects left behind by its late owner, Saul—Zohara's uncle. He was some kind of artist, Zohara had once told me. A lonesome man plagued by memories of war. She neglected to inform me that he had, not so long ago, taken his own life right there in the toolshed. She must have been afraid that would make me think less of the house that her parents had given us as a wedding gift—legitimizing, at least outwardly, our marriage, which I had always suspected was not to their liking.

And so, only on the night they handed over the keys, as we made our way to the shed in the backyard, did Zohara's father tell me about the noose the deceased owner had hung from an iron beam in the ceiling. Did he also perceive his brother-in-law's actions as a rebellion against the arbitrariness of life? I hoped so, but found it hard to believe that a thought like that would indeed dwell in the orderly mind of such a pragmatic man.

"Come," he told me, "you'll like it." I followed my father-in-law down a narrow concrete path that squeezed its way between the ratty façade of the house and the tangled thorns that had taken over the yard. They were thick-stemmed, and most of them reached above our shoulders. At the edge of the plot, a nocturnal wind cooed among the dark screen of trees, and the thorns replied in a threatening whisper.

Now, hunching, I walked backward, raising the branches above my lowered head with my left hand, as I dragged the table by its leg with my right. I pulled it toward me, plowing a furrow through the carpet of leaves. A glance at the shorn yard behind my back startled my heart, as if I'd just witnessed a body with a missing limb.

I set the table on its legs. Then, with an affected industriousness, I evaded Zohara's gaze and wriggled into the thicket to fetch the chairs.

The sun vanished from sight, leaving the remains of its dwindling light behind. Zohara stood tall, hands on her hips, pregnant belly prominent in her nightgown, pointing a foot in the direction of my journey with the wooden chairs, from the thicket to the table, which—at her behest—I later moved a little farther from the house, to the shade of the pecan tree. Zohara stood tall, hands on her hips, pregnant belly prominent in her nightgown, pointing a foot in the direction of my journey with the wooden chairs, from the thicket to the table, which—at her behest—I later moved a little farther from the house, to the shade of the pecan tree.

My chair wobbled as I sat on it, responding to every little shift I made with a pronounced squeak. The light that beamed from the kitchen window went out, and in the dimness, I recognized the tinkle of ice cubes in the glass growing louder. Going by the music of the ice, I could picture her bare feet pacing carefully across the raked ground until, finally, she bent down behind me to place a steaming cup on the table. Then she passed before me in her sky-blue nightgown, moving with that same skipping step, almost exactly as I'd pictured her, and took a seat on the other side of the table. She sipped from the tall glass, in which ice cubes hissed. She sighed, and then, as our eyes met, smiled and set the glass down with a tap.

"You know, Guri, right here, just a little closer to the tree, where it's almost completely dark right now," she said, turning her face away before returning it to me, "I thought we could put an inflatable pool for her."

"What if it's a boy?"

"Boys like water too, don't they? Except then I'd have to look for a different pool than the one I saw."

"In your imagination?"

"No, at the store."

I took a small sip. The coffee was rich and more flavorful than all those questionable hot beverages I'd consumed during my watch for Yaara. And yet, the memory of the tea I'd had at the old man's apartment, which had stung my throat either due to its temperature or its sweetness—I still wasn't sure—inspired a certain longing. Most likely for the state of mind I was in when I still believed it was only a short journey until our coveted reunion, and the Yaara I would meet still appeared to me as that light-limbed doe who had climbed into the bus on Ahuza Street all those years ago, riding away from me.

The heavy clay mug in my hand was thick and cream-colored on the outside, and its weight often misled the hand with regard to its contents. It landed heavily on the table, and the moment I let go of the handle, Zohara caught my eye, and told me she'd found a baby supply store within walking distance of her office, and that sometimes she went there during her lunch break... that's where she had seen that marshmallow-pink inflatable pool… her colleague Osnat was also pregnant, but she was already… and knew she was having…

It seemed that, at this point, Zohara's words became completely garbled in my ears, and I was aware only of the movement of her lips, which, in the bluish moonlight, disguised and revealed the glistening moisture brushed across her front teeth, small as baby teeth. I felt a closeness, then shame… Most powerful of all was the guilt toward the fetus in her womb. Both of them were perceived in my mind as abandoned, merely due to my thoughts of abandonment, which were exacerbated, along with my urge to fan the smoldering logs of my past.

Zohara sipped on her iced coffee. A round pebble of ice slipped into her mouth, and she crushed it between her teeth. Then she spoke some more, telling me about her job in detail. As I listened, I nodded along, occasionally contributing my opinion in a few words, taking a quick sip now and then, and setting aside my mug.

As the minutes passed, foam marks ringed the inside of my mug, and I pictured myself climbing up Zohara's success to the height of an elegant fortress, from which I could look down at the emptiness of my own life.

Eventually, Zohara got to her feet, eyes lighting up with a bizarre desire. As she approached me with a seductive step, she shifted her eyes between me and some faraway point beyond my right shoulder. At the same time, twisting her hips teasingly, she slowly lowered her panties under the nightgown. When she finally handed them to me, there was something sweet and mean about her gaze.

I turned back, without thinking, in the direction where I suspected whoever had fueled her desire could be found. In the window on the second floor of the neighboring house, the silhouette of a man watched us through the cracks between shutters. I pictured Yuval standing there, his hand down his pants, caressing Zohara with his eyes. I wanted to stop this debauchery, but Zohara was already squeezing her knee between my legs, the edges of her lips curling into a smile of crude pleasure.

She needed an onlooker to watch so she could feel the extent of her existence. When she'd brought herself to the edge of this possibility, a savage lust rocked her body. A thread of curiosity drew me once more to the events taking place behind me, but Zohara was already on my lap, gyrating wildly, tossing off her nightgown. The chair creaked below me. For a flash, I noticed her translucent eyelashes fluttering in the direction of Yuval. I slipped my hand between her burning thighs, and she gasped. I loosened my pants, and, with a vengeful urge, pushed into her.

I lingered on the garden chair in sad fatigue. My breathing was still heavy, and I was too exhausted to even zip up. From the edge of our yard, the chirping sharpened in my ears. Behind my shoulder, darkness fell over the house, and Zohara walked toward it softly along the raked dirt, her white arm away from her body, holding her small underwear by the tips of her fingers, as if it belonged to a stranger.

For a while longer, I stared at the patch of earth Zohara had left behind. When I heard the muffled sounds of the shower starting, I turned away from the wall, my chair screeching—a submissive screech, compared to its vigorous protestations only moments ago.

In times of intimacy, Zohara swore to me over and over again that her craving for a stranger's gaze took nothing away from her desire for me. She had defined this urge coursing through her body when she was a young teen. And indeed, when the storm passed, Zohara always fell into my arms like a trembling baby bird. Her quick heartbeat would pulsate from her hot, sweaty skin to my hairy chest, and I would hold her until her chills dwindled and confidence returned to me. But this night, my faith in her was shaken.

I trundled inside and could still hear the shower water gliding down her body and down the floor tiles beneath her feet. It lasted a few moments longer before the stream was cut off, dying inside the pipe. I was afraid that Zohara would step outside at any moment, and I would have to look her in the eyes from within my inextricable thicket of emotion.

My head was buried under the blanket on our bed, and I inhaled my own breath. My attention wandered between thoughts of the deed we'd done in the yard and the sketching of Zohara's movements in my mind, relying on sounds that filtered through from the bathroom. As was her custom, she spent a long time moisturizing her body, then padded through the hallway. When she opened the bedroom door, I pretended to be asleep.

I sensed her lingering in the doorway, but she didn't come in. I pictured her wrapped in a white bathrobe, turning on the television in the living room, and sitting down to watch.

Cheeks aflame, I poked my head out of the blanket. My body was somewhat relieved. But my wrath at Zohara had not subsided, still darkening my mood. Without noticing, I'd slipped into old thought patterns; the details of my youth, which had been composed of hours of loneliness and inferiority, bubbled up to my conscious mind, bending and twisting my adult form, until I felt the need for a maternal shoulder to cry on once more.

It's surprising that, until the moment when I took a closer look at the photograph, I had not remembered that Yaara was at my grandmother's home while my leg wounds were being sanitized. I wondered whether this formative event, etched in my mind as a one-time occurrence, had, in fact, recurred several times before my mother finally broke down. Did Yaara remember me crying with pain, then witnessing my mother's anguish, choking down tears, and settling myself? What did she think of me then, seeing me agonizing under the nurse's care?

Finally, I made up my mind. With a shaking hand, I pulled the third photograph from between the folds of the paper and looked. In the picture, my father is sitting on the living room couch in Eldad and Noga's wood-paneled house. He's wearing a white Polo shirt and slacks, raising a cup of coffee in his large hand to his lips, his head lowered a tad. I'm about six years old, standing by his right foot, placing a dimpled hand on his knee. Blond bangs cover my forehead, and my innocent eyes look up at my father, my expression projecting complete faith.

Once again, my wheelchair strode down Oliphant Street, my grandmother restraining it with the strength of her arms, until we slowed down at the tiled plane by the entrance to her apartment block. As usual, she parked me in the lobby. "Wait here," she said, then climbed slowly up a short flight of stairs, knocked twice, and then once more, louder this time, on a brown door with a protruding peephole, quickly fixing her hair with her fingers before it opened.

The doorway was crowded by a rumple-haired man with broad shoulders and large hands. He glanced at me awkwardly and stepped outside silently, as if he had no choice but to acquiesce. Leaving my grandmother with her back to the wall, he took the stairs down to meet me.

Only weeks earlier, my mother had left the apartment, knocked meekly upon this door, and asked for his help for the first time. The first I knew of it was his appearance at our door. He carried my wheelchair down three floors, one step at a time. Echoing thwacks and, the metallic ringing of each step resonated through the building, reaching me as I lay on my linen-covered couch. Minutes later, the man returned to us, breathless, looking about him as if disoriented, emitting a quick, "Oh," that signified he had noticed my mother, then following her into the living room. He carried me in his arms from the couch to the door, while my frazzled mother sprayed his stooped back with trite compliments. His sour breath hummed in my ears, warming the gap between my nostrils and the itchy stubble on his neck throughout our descent, until finally, he placed me back in my wheelchair, and I could breathe a sigh of relief.

In the days that had gone by since, my mother had barely left the apartment. Eventually, she even stopped taking me out on my afternoon stroll. Grandma took her place, and treated the generous neighbor like a servant. If that wasn't bad enough, his quick response to her knocking made me think that perhaps all he did all day was sit in a chair in the dark next to his door, awaiting our arrival.

—

In her few visits to our home, the nurse instructed me on how to sanitize my wounds by myself. Mom had relieved herself of this duty, which she'd failed to perform properly in the first place, due to the pity she took on me. But this morning, when I awakened on the made couch, I didn't find the bandaging supplies on the coffee table beside me. The soft dawn light filtering in through the shutters dimly lit a patch of a nearby wall, as well as the ratty carpet. I sailed my eyes up and down the living room until I caught sight of a tender glow on the smooth face of a brown glass bottle. The other accouterments were set around it on the edge of a square table in the corner between the couches. It was as if, last night, while I was asleep under a floral summer blanket whose folds disguised the shape of my body, Mom and Grandma shifted and camouflaged every last ugly object that had anything to do with me, including creams and ointments smelling of pharmaceutical ill health—the smell that had clung to my skin long ago.

For a while, I had been hearing the tinkling of dishes and smelling the aromas of *Bourikas* baking from my grandmother's kitchen, but now I feared that if I asked her for help again, she would criticize my mother for locking herself in her childhood bedroom while the sanitation was taking place, rather than staying with me.

In my physical state, I couldn't roll over onto my stomach, so instead, I used the walker to help me up and edged slowly to the end of the couch, where, carefully, I stood up on my healthy leg, and, crane-like, transferred all of the instruments from the low table in the corner onto the glass plate of the coffee table. After a few more complicated maneuvers, I lay down on my side on the couch, my breathing shallow. Whenever I pressed the hydrogen peroxide-dipped cotton swabs into the wounds on the side of my hip, the pain seared, and I bit my lips.

The soft click of a lock informed me that my mother had stepped out of her room just as I had completed the most painful stage in the process. I began applying red antiseptic ointment as she moved into the bathroom, and when she came out, I listened intently, hoping she would come my way. Instead, I heard a chair dragging in the kitchen, followed by the muffled sounds of conversation. My grandmother's voice assaulted her at the pace of a military march, and my mother's response rose like a wind sighing through the foliage.

Once, my mother told me that, while I lay in my hospital bed, she used to disobey the nurses by lying beside me. Even though I was unconscious, she couldn't bear my loneliness. Now, I pulled my pants up over my wounds, making sure that the tips of the four metal rods that stuck out of my left thigh were poking through the perforations in the dark fabric.

The living-room carpet dulled the tapping of the walker, but as I descended to the floor tiles on my way to the kitchen, each of my steps began with a loud whacking sound and the jingling of metal. I pictured my mother and grandmother sharing a look. *Here he comes.*

I can't remember what words my mother used to welcome me into the kitchen, which was filled with the aroma of frying, but I remember the exhausted smile that pulled on one side of her lips, and the reddish rings around her sockets as she rested her eyes on me, tracking my every movement until I sat down. Then she sipped her coffee and ate slowly, keeping her eyes on the fork she used to cut up her omelet.

"Well, if you're already sitting down, you might as well eat." Grandma pointed her metal spatula toward me while a pan sizzled on the stove behind her. I can't remember if I was hungry, but before I could even answer, she advanced toward me. "Here, I made this plate for myself," she said. She placed a plate of greasy omelets on the round table and turned to face the range. Another egg was cracked, its contents inciting a new riot in the frying pan.

I pushed my chest against the side of the table and dragged the plate over noisily. Mom didn't bat an eye.

Her hair shaded her thin profile, emphasizing her bitter, unfamiliar features. But tiny twitches attested to a stealthy journey of the mind, cracking her mask of mourning. I was drawn to the meaning of these as if by invisible webs, until I'd forgotten all about the omelet.

The silverware drawer opened and closed with a rattling. As if wishing to tear me away from my reveries, my grandmother came up behind me and dropped a knife and fork beside my plate, a gesture that I took as criticism for staring at my mother. Now, her back to us, she ran a wet rag over the patch of counter between the stovetop and the sink, then folded the rag and placed it on the side of the sink. She washed her hands and dried them with a towel, which she rubbed vigorously up and down her fingers with their burgundy-painted nails. The entire time, I could hear her moist breaths like waves crashing in the dark, growing louder as she approached. She smacked her plate against the table, containing a yellow omelet folded into a perfect semi-circle, then dragged over a chair and took a seat to my left, leaving a gap between us, wide enough for an extra person.

"Aren't you eating?" she asked, passing an oval bowl of pink fish and slices of onions swimming in golden oil under my nose. I shook my head, and she pulled the bowl back and served herself a hefty portion, then handed it to my mother, who twisted her face at it.

Grandma sighed defiantly, plopped a spoonful of cream cheese onto her plate, salted everything, and cut a piece of omelet. She chewed on it, angling quizzical looks at her daughter, then swallowed and took up another forkful. She chewed with growing impatience, until finally she exploded at Mom. "What's wrong?!" Her intonation left no room for a response.

Mom flinched, and a look of panic froze on her face. Grandma, who had yet to internalize what she'd caused with her words, wiped cheese spray from the corner of her lips and chewed what was left in her mouth. Tears filled my mother's eyes, and sobs burbled from her throat, choked and broken. Her state had weighed heavily on me for a long time, because even when she was able to restrain her tears, she continued to sniffle like an indulgent baby, hands shaking on the table.

Grandma, who until this moment behaved as one whose Saturday morning tranquility had been disrupted, now softened and reached a hand over to Mom. But when she tried to take it, their palms wrestled like a pair of naked mole rats on the table until Mom pulled hers away, let out a spiteful chuckle, and wiped her eyes.

Grandma closed her freckled hands around the edge of the table, rose with a disgruntled groan, walked to the cabinet, and quickly returned with a handful of burgundy paper napkins.

The doorbell rang. "Who is it now?" she grumbled, turning away from the faucet.

Mom crumpled a napkin into a doughy lump and placed it among the food scraps on her plate. She got to her feet, lost in reveries. Another chirp, more persistent this time, came from the buzzer, urging her to get to the door.

"What a special guest!" she said when she opened it, her voice lilting childishly.

This "special guest" was hidden from view by my mother's back in her faded floral nightgown and the darkness behind the half-open door. I wanted so badly to get to the door, but by the time I got off my seat and advanced over with my walker, the door closed. In the hallway, my mother smiled at me with tight lips, her eyes seeming to conceal a secret. In retrospect, I thought she hesitated for a moment, as if looking for the easiest way out. Then she revealed to me that Yaara, the daughter of a neighbor across the way, had come over to invite me to go with her and her father to see a movie.

I asked if I was allowed to.

"Do you want to?" Mom replied, tilting her head slightly. The way she spoke the words—slowly, like two separate questions—attested to the reservations she'd detected in my voice. I did want to, but my hesitation to rely on Yaara's father for close assistance during our stay in the cinema was matched by my embarrassment about revealing my feelings for the girl to my mother.

"What's on your mind? You look worried."

"A little."

"Well?" Her eyebrows arched, and she bit her lip with anticipation.

"No, I want to," I said with determination. Though I knew my mother tended to avoid any activity she thought might pose a risk to me, I presented my wishes to her. Before she could even answer, my imagination carried me away from the marks my mother's teeth were left on her lips to the seats of the movie theater. I pictured Yaara's dark eyes flickering in the lights of the screen, riveted to the film, while I was riveted by her high forehead.

"Have you forgotten about tonight?" my grandmother intervened from the kitchen. My mother's expression turned. She looked quizzically behind my back. "You and Ami have plans."

"Oh! I forgot all about that. But I'd hate for Gur to miss out."

"What?"

"Hang on, we don't need to shout," Mom said.

I turned the walker to follow her, dragging myself in her wake silently, trying not to draw attention to myself.

When Mom reached the kitchen doorway, she said, "You know, I wanted him to have a little break." She crossed her skinny arms against her chest so tightly that I couldn't see her elbows from behind.

"Oh, well," Grandma muttered, "we go to the garden every day."

"I'll just call. Maybe Ami can come by earlier to help him get ready."

Grandma removed her dripping rubber gloves and turned to face my mother. Her forehead screwed up. "Ami? Come on. He's got enough on his mind without having to bathe your son."

"My son? He isn't doing me any favors, Mother."

"Still…"
Mom sighed, her arms dropping to her sides.

"We shouldn't take advantage," Grandma concluded.

I was plagued with doubts. Ami was my mother's distant cousin, a thirty-year-old laborer for whom, for some unknown reason, our tragedy struck some obscure chord among the fortifications of his soul. Had we gotten him involved in a commitment he was no longer interested in?

"I'm wiped," Mom grunted.

Silence descended over the apartment. The only sounds were the footfalls of my grandma's slippers and the dull thump of a large fruit bowl she placed at the center of the table, a sign that her work was done. Mom turned her head back, eyes widening, as if she'd just remembered I was there, bearing witness. I feared I'd burden her with my worries, so I lowered my eyes. Below the walker, I saw my healthy foot treading on the polished floor in an old sock, and my wounded leg bent at the knee. Once again, I was enveloped with an odd sense of distance, a lack of ownership over my own body.

Only late in the afternoon did my mother walk over to the couch where I lay and suggest I prepare for Ami's arrival. That's when I realized the weakness I'd detected in her voice that morning was merely a retreat from the heart of the conflict with her mother, and that, ultimately, she made sure I could go to the movies with Yaara.

—

Ami supported me as I undressed, hanging my clothes and helping me over the side of the bathtub. Then he walked back and examined his unshaven face in the mirror over the sink, angling the occasional supervising look in my direction. After a long pause, he noticed me lingering under the dry showerhead and pleaded, "Come on!"—his tone more masculine and impatient than I'd ever heard from him before.

I felt humiliated. Why was I paralyzed, not turning on the water stream even as the skin of my arms and thighs pimpled with cold? Was there a part of me that secretly hoped Ami would bathe me, soaping my body with his large hands, just like he did when I was still in the wheelchair?

I leaned my left hand against the brown porcelain walls, turned on the water, and drew the curtain. The jingling of the curtain rings as they slid across the rod brought up a brief memory from the curtain around my hospital bed, the drawing of which portended pain.

—

I sat on the couch wearing a polo shirt and wide slacks, counting down the minutes until seven o'clock. I pictured myself as a rough, pleasant man, like the stars of Saturday-night movies on TV. In my high spirits, I longed to be the one to greet Yaara at the door. For the moment, nothing but a bluish deep-sea light and a humming wind invaded the apartment through the open balcony doors, as Mom and Grandma sat at the balcony table, silently sipping cold coffee from tall glasses tinkling with ice cubes. The heavy ticking of the clock on the kitchen wall reverberated loudly through the apartment, like a heavy brass pendulum slowly swinging back and forth, rather than its simple, slender marching hands.

Shortly after the agreed-upon time, Yigal, Yaara's father, showed up at the door. A straight-backed man with his shoulders drawn, his face the color of chestnuts, and his red beard stood out against his black clothes. He sensed my embarrassment, quickly ducked down to align his face with mine, and informed me that Yaara was waiting for us downstairs.

"Oh, wonderful," Mom sighed and giggled awkwardly from inside the dim apartment as if attempting to conceal something.

Yigal swallowed and leaned against the doorframe. He waited for me to cross the threshold and returned to crushing a lock of his beard with his hand.

When I reached the stairs, I glanced at him again. He was still standing under the hallway fuse box, legs crossed, chatting with my mother, who was standing just inside the doorway. I decided not to wait and took the stairs down slowly. Though I was nervous, my muscles shaking with the effort, an elemental part of me was still striving for independence.

I remembered how much my grandmother resented this man. How she always referred to him as a "low-rent Don Juan." I hoped my mother still liked him and that their lingering conversation was not a burden to her. I was so afraid that Mom would weaken and I would lose her too, that I had become attuned to the tiniest shifts in her expression and tone of voice.

Each sign of discomfort contained an insinuation of the next disaster.

I heard footsteps coming down the stairs behind me, advancing with the hasty tapping of thin-soled shoes. I was worried Yigal would crash into me and wanted to quicken my steps, but I was afraid to stumble. His name was already ready on my tongue, prepared for a warning cry if no other option remained, but to my relief, I heard him slowing down. He paused at the landing right above me, and when I'd gotten enough distance from him, he followed me with measured steps.

Yaara wasn't waiting at the bottom of the stairs as I'd expected. Instead, she stood with her back to us by the front door, which shone in the twilight. Her hair rolled down her shoulders, and a pleated black skirt exposed the backs of her knees. I cannot recall what else she wore that night, but it was most likely a mélange of clothing that appeared to have been pulled out of a costume trunk, affording her "formal" attire with a nomadic shabbiness.

We waited at the corner until her father returned in his wine-colored Ford Cortina, which he maneuvered quickly, pulling up beside us. He stepped out of the car, engine still running, and opened the back door with a gracious flourish.

"How do you usually get in, Gur?"

"From the front?"

"This is a wide car. What do you think? Can you get in the back?"

"I think so."

"Great. We don't want any trouble with the police, do we?"

Yigal held the door open while I advanced toward it. Meanwhile, darkness thickened around us, and I was convinced I'd make us late for the movie. A yellowish light spread through the cab of the car like dust through the air, shining against muscular leather seats, as red as a rooster's crest.

"Need any help?" Yaara's voice came up behind me at just the right moment, imbuing me with a certain peace. I moved a little closer, turned my back on the car, and sat down carefully on the edge of the seat. I pulled my body along the backseat with my left leg stretched out in front of me. In the meantime, Yigal picked up my walker and closed it in the trunk with a tinny thunk.

Yaara watched me from the sidewalk until I could place my injured leg between the front seats. "Hang on," she said once I was settled, "I'll get in from the other side. I don't want to hurt you." She straightened, walked around the trunk, and soon sat beside me.

Yaara watched me from the sidewalk until I could place my injured leg between the front seats.

"Hang on," she said, once I was settled, "I'll get in from the other side. I don't want to hurt you."

She straightened, walked around the trunk, and soon sat beside me.

"Are you guys crowded back there?"

"A little bit," Yaara replied mischievously. She leaned over me and slammed the door shut with a momentum that pushed her back against the seat. The car smelled of greased steel and cheap shaving cream. I looked around, but besides an empty Coke can squished next to the handbrake and used as an ashtray, I saw no evidence of life.

Yigal squeezed through metallic groans of increasing intensity from the motor, put the car in drive, and accelerated up the street. Our heads pressed against the seatbacks, and the wind howled through the windows. Yaara's hair whipped against my face, and I realized that our bodies were flush against each other from shoulder to thigh.

The car suddenly slowed down, then carried on in fits and spurts among traffic lights and illuminated intersections.

"Do you know what movie we're going to see?" Yaara asked.

"No," I said.

"That's funny."

"What?"

"The fact that you don't know. What if it's a horror movie? What would you do then?"

"I could close my eyes."

"Wouldn't that be a waste?" Yaara shrugged and turned her profile toward me. I watched the city lights twinkling against her eyelashes and was worried she'd lost interest in me.

The engine growled. Yigal worked the stick with a determined arm adorned with fuzzy ginger hair. We sped down a slope, the wind wilding from the two open front windows. A black sea opened up before us, strewn with the flickering of freight ships making their way to and from the port. Yaara's hair flew in the wind, whipping my face harder as we sped on. Yigal's right hand now held onto the steering wheel while his left arm rested along the window, so the odds he would roll it up seemed slim.

As Yaara's hair whipped around, I suddenly became aware of the warmth of her body along my naked arm, and then I carefully attempted to release it away.

"You're in pain!" Yaara wasn't upset but rather prepared, as if having been waiting on alert for the moment I needed her.

"No, your hair is just getting in my mouth," I said, softening my voice as I spoke. I'd only wanted to remove irritation from between my lips, but now I found my arm stretched over the headrest, trapped behind Yaara's head. I couldn't remember when and how I'd put it there. My other arm was blocked by hers.

"Look, it's like you have a mustache!" Yaara held a long lock of her hair over my lips, examining me with gravity until dimples finally appeared on her cheeks. I shook my head in objection, and she laughed teasingly. "All right, okay, I'll stop."

She looked away, the scent of her breaths dying in my nose.

I noticed that the landscape outside the windows had changed, and I felt as if I were waking up in the eye of a storm. The lights of the highway flashed barrages into the car. Yigal turned up the volume on the radio and leaned back, while Yaara lowered her head as if dipping her hair in a dark pail.

Down her bent back, I noticed that same delicate shawl that had fallen off her shoulders. Then she raised her body up, one vertebra at a time, hands on her forehead, elbows bent like a submissive soldier. Biting my lips, I watched as she slowly smoothed her hair. A flash of light revealed the swell of her breasts underneath her shirt, and I dropped my gaze into the dimness, paused in embarrassment, and then looked between the seats again, slowly. Her father switched gears, then returned his hand to the wheel.

Had Yaara caught my glance? Had our feelings intersected? She remained sitting upright for a long moment, tied her hair back, and said, "Dad, aren't we going to be late?"

—

An usher led us with the beam of his flashlight toward our row of seats. Yaara walked with him, while Yigal followed slowly behind me. The tapping of my walker against the theater floor attracted many pairs of eyes, watching me over the backs of the red upholstered seats. I felt mortified. I wanted to yell, "This isn't me! I'm not really disabled!"

A young woman stood up and pulled her little boy to his feet, moving into the aisle to let us into their row. Yaara angled her body around and slipped through the tight space with the litheness of a mongoose, making her way between seats and stubborn knees. She left an empty seat to her left and sat down, adjusting the shawl around her shoulders and looking up at me with questioning eyes. I think it was only then that she realized I wasn't able to wriggle in after her.

Meanwhile, Yigal was conversing with a young usher in a hushed whisper, crushing the same lock of his beard he had fiddled with when he'd stood in the doorway of my grandmother's apartment talking to my mom. I spent an agonizing minute standing awkwardly until the usher, and Yigal led me—under the watchful gaze of dozens of curious eyes—to a seat in the front row. Slowly, I lowered myself down, letting Yigal help me lean the heel of my outstretched leg on the bar of the walker he'd placed beside me.

In the middle of the movie, Yaara sneaked into the seat next to mine. Her movements were sharp, and her expression was annoyed. Our eyes met, and she let out a stifled whisper: "Ugh! He's so irritating!"

"Who is?"

"My father! He left after a second and disappeared for like an hour." Her anger seemed sharper, the edges of her words piercing through the cover of her whisper.

"When? Just now?"

"No, earlier, at intermission. When he came back, he was acting all weird. I feel like…" There was a tremble in her voice.

"Go on," I whispered. "Tell me."

"You know, like he…" Yaara interrupted herself with a deep breath as if wishing to inhale back the thoughts.

"Say it."

"Never mind, it's nonsense. Really." Her eyes evaded mine. Suddenly, she asked, "Gur, does this shawl look good on me?" She tossed the fabric over her shoulder and turned to face me with a graceful gesture, her dainty, summery face flickering with the lights from the screen in the moving darkness.

I yearned to praise it out loud, but my throat wouldn't allow me to. Instead, I just nodded.

"It's nice and soft too," she added. "Feel it. No, not like that. Give me your cheek. See?"

I caught only a whiff of the intoxicating fragrance of the thin fabric held in her confident, indulgent fingers before someone behind us shushed us. I looked straight ahead at the screen to conceal my bashfulness. For a while, we sat as still as two strangers, until suddenly Yaara placed a cool finger on my forehead.

I froze. With a tender caress, she ran her finger along the contour of an indented scar that twisted down the right side of my forehead. I swallowed, aware of my hastening breath at the motion of her finger as it sailed along the brow of my injured eye, then descended very slowly down my nose and between my lips. My heart pounded. Yaara pulled down my scarred lower lip with a stiff finger, touching the exposed damp area. I felt her brave eyes against my skin but didn't dare look her way.

Her inflamed eyes, peering over high cheekbones, and her graceful body, enchanted me—perhaps because they stood in stark opposition to my scarred face and wounded body. I often wondered, with envy, how it felt to own such a disciplined figure.

To this day, oddly, when I recall Yaara's athletic robustness, I am reminded of the impression left on me by my own body during the final summer of my village childhood—when the last rays of evening sun twinkled along the water of the public pool, most bathers already standing on the lawn, wrapped in towels, their hair dripping. Some were gathering their belongings in preparation for the walk home. In contrast, others sprawled out on lounge chairs and mats among friends and family for a time longer, eating watermelon and homemade sandwiches, enjoying a rare breeze.

While my friends and I raced each other in the now-vacant pool, each time I lifted my right arm and popped my head out for air, the sight of my biceps tightening against the sun filled me with pride—a sign of early adolescence.

On our way back from the movie theater, Yaara squeezed into her seat, chewing and releasing her lips, as if carrying on a furious argument with herself, occasionally pausing to fix the back of her father's head with charged glares. Many minutes went by before she finally demanded an explanation. "Dad, who was that woman you went outside with?"

"Oh, that one? Beats me. We both wanted a smoke, so we left the theater together."

"But you were outside for so long," Yaara protested in a tone unfamiliar to me.

"The important thing is that you got your popcorn, isn't it?"

Yaara fell silent, leaning her head against the window. Her father sniffed loudly and turned on the radio. Now, a sense of distress rested over us, and I felt pangs of conscience, thinking that perhaps, in my absence, they might have been able to break the tension more easily. The wind rustled through a crack in the window while Yaara's breathing deepened and settled with every passing moment. Finally, during one of the car's turns, her body slowly shifted toward me, her head dropping against my shoulder. Free to look, I spent a long time gazing at her closed eyelids and her innocent, slightly parted lips. Then, gradually, I came to the mute conclusion that, just like me, Yaara was still a child.

An unfamiliar ashtray and two glasses rested on the balcony table. Both chairs had been moved to the table's corner—a testament to an intimate conversation. I saw my mother's friend Sofia leaning against the railing, smoking, lost in thought. Between inhalation and exhalation, she ran her thumbnail over her top lip. She was so focused that she didn't even hear the door opening. By the time she noticed us, Grandma and I had been standing on the edge of the rug for quite a while, watching her as she dwelled in her own world.

"Oh, hello! One moment, I'll be right there." She crushed her cigarette in the ashtray and ran a hand through her hair. Picking up the ashtray, she walked over, shrouded in mystery. "She's sleeping now," she told my grandmother in an affected whisper, emphasizing the last word, charging all that had preceded this sleep with ominous meaning.

Grandma nodded gravely. "That's better." Her soft voice and expression concerned me. I recalled how determined she'd been to get me out of the apartment about two hours ago, and all at once, the details of our trip to the zoo, along with the ice cream she'd bought me there, came together to form an awkward ruse. The realization melted away any ownership I had felt over my life following my movie theater outing with Yaara the previous night.

Sofia was too frenetic for me to catch her eye. She quickly left the living room, and in an instant, we heard her emptying the ashtray into the sink and running the water. Was she avoiding me? Or was she merely acting out of the knowledge that my grandmother abhorred smoking and was in an anxious hurry to prove she wouldn't be leaving a mess behind?

Lately, my mother's energy had dwindled, and she rarely left her room. As a result, Grandma had spent the past few days pacing the apartment, mumbling complaints, until, just the previous night, she'd changed her tune and defended my mother against me. She watched me like a hawk, ensuring I didn't come near my mother's door. Whenever she caught me lurking, I burned with rage. Outwardly, I kept my cool. But on my way back to the couch, when the blush of fury diminished, my anger mixed with guilt, the two emotions thickening to brew a distress that stayed with me for hours. Whenever I wished optimistically for my mother's recovery, I grew appalled by my own blasé attitude, intentionally underestimating every comforting ray of light.

Before she left, Sofia exchanged a few quiet words with Grandma. Then she knelt before me, tilted her head, looked into my eyes, and asked, "And how are you, Gur?"

I didn't answer, but I still recall her soft voice and a dark curve in her semi-translucent stockings, along which her thigh pressed against her calf.

—

I opened the door and saw a dark lump nestled in the narrow bed in the corner of the room. As I approached it slowly, my pupils adjusted to the dimness. My mother's hand emerged to pull the blanket over her head. She wrapped herself tighter back to me, resembling a frightened animal.

I whispered "Mom" repeatedly until her body shifted under the blanket. She turned over slowly and poked her head out from between the folds. "Are you all right, Gur?" Her words reached me in a voice that reminded me of different, more faraway days. Her eyes protruded over her sunken cheeks. She could barely keep them open, though a hint of a smile twitched on her lips.

—

I spent long moments lying on the couch, my eyes fixed on the living room ceiling, agonizing over the paralysis of my tongue I'd experienced in my mother's presence. Her eyes had projected grief and worry, as well as a long tunnel leading toward a lost life. I was afraid of losing her and felt an urge to return to her room and save her from her heartbreak. While Grandma was out of the apartment a few times, I mustered the courage to break the hush, slowly clinking my walker along the corridor toward Mom's door. I would open a crack and peek through the dimness at the fabric cocoon, watching until I saw it rising and falling almost imperceptibly, and heard the rustle of her breath.

One hot Saturday, late afternoon, Grandma walked into the dark room, practical and assertive. I heard the blinds being pulled up with broken spurts and saw a blazing trapezoid of light stretching from the doorway up the opposite wall. Grandma spoke decisively, with only some pauses and changes in tone, bookending the spaces in which my mother may have talked back.

I waited, eavesdropping, for an excruciating spell before a long shadow fell along the wall, and Mom walked out of the room, soft and slumped, wearing the floral nightgown that hung off her shoulders as if from a clothes hanger. Possessively, Grandma followed her down the hall, resting a heavy palm on Mom's shoulder as they entered the kitchen, steering her toward the table.

My back to the fridge, I watched Mom's delayed, effortful movements, as if this were the first time she'd ever pulled out a chair in her life. While she sat down, Grandma ladled out the contents of a wide, stained aluminum pot on the stove, filling a bowl with chicken soup dotted with all manner of root vegetables.

"I used the carrots you like," she said.

Mom responded with a nod. From the corner of her eye, she caught my concerned expression and returned a faint smile. Then she stared at me, remote, as if gripped by some intrusive thought.

I walked over to the cabinet and pulled out a dark chocolate bar. I knew to avoid the soul-bending battle between the two women. I was so fearful of the moments it erupted outwardly that I kept my distance even when a tense tranquility existed between them. I broke off a piece of chocolate and bit into it. In the seconds it took to melt in my mouth, Grandma turned from the table to the corner of the counter, where she sliced a loaf of bread with a long knife.

Mom picked up her spoon languidly and leaned toward the table to sip the soup. With every spoonful she swallowed, her appetite seemed to grow. She even brought her face closer to the bowl and crossed her legs under the seat.

As I walked out, I lingered in the doorway, glancing back with anticipation. But Mom's eyes were preoccupied. Her spoon now rested at the greasy bottom of the bowl. She conversed with Grandma in a low voice, using the breaks between speech to bite on a piece of buttered bread.

The picture Bible I'd perused the previous night before going to sleep was still on the living room table. I sat on the couch and flipped through it distractedly until I heard my mother's bare feet padding over. There were long pauses between each step. After the footsteps stopped, the bathroom door slammed, then slammed again, as if it had a faulty latch.

From the day I could think and feel, my mother taught me that bathing was an elixir against foul moods. And so, when she got out of bed and showered after such a long respite in darkness, hope bloomed in my heart. But from the moment Mom began to extricate herself from the cocoon of her sorrow, her movements broadened every day until, finally, she left me behind to fend for myself against the burden of my injury and the malicious changes to my body, before I could even muster the strength and bravery to grieve my father's death.

My mother's near-lustful need to generate meaningful change in our lives was one of those phenomena whose significance I barely perceived as it occurred. But I knew she feared that if we tried to recreate the same routine we'd had during my father's life, living in the village, we would be stepping on shards of broken memory wherever we turned.

Occasionally, I overheard the details of plans she and Sofia made over extended phone calls, between sobs, chuckles of sarcasm, and painful acceptance. Once, I heard Mom say, "That's possible. If we can find a nice apartment there, not too far from you…"

The next evening, Mom opened an elongated black suitcase on the living room table. From crevices of blue velvet, she patiently pulled out the three silver parts of a flute. She polished them with a soft fabric, then screwed them together, meticulously checking the joints and keys, as well as the layer of felt covering it all. When she finished, she sighed with rare satisfaction, got up from her chair, and walked straight to the window. She filled her lungs with air, placed the flute's mouthpiece in the dimple of her chin, and played a piece I was familiar with, named *Afternoon of a Faun*. Just like I used to before the disaster, I listened attentively for her soft, quick breaths between the notes.

Before my father died, Mom taught music three times a week at the conservatory in Haifa. One day a week, she audited a musicology class at the university. Apart from homemaking, Mom spent most of her time within the confines of a musical bubble she'd formed for herself, inside of which I imagined she felt protected against the unrelenting difficulty of life.

———

One day, my village classmates Ayelet and Tamir visited me at Grandma's. While Mom welcomed them affectionately, I looked down at my body, framed by the walker. For a moment, I wondered what people were saying about us back in the village and what I must have looked like now to my friends. I glanced at them bashfully. A curly-haired woman and a mustachioed man stood in the doorway behind them, whom I recognized as Ayelet's parents. They exchanged greetings with my mother. When they asked how I was doing, she answered for me. She led them into the kitchen while my friends headed to the living room. I slowly followed them with my walker, its knocking absorbed by the ragged carpet.

Ayelet bunched up the train of her yellow dress as she moved between the glass table and the made-up couch. She sat down on the loveseat and looked me over with marvel as I slowly lowered myself onto the couch. I caught a hint of revulsion in her eyes, imagined the emotions my wounded body must have inspired in her, and flinched inwardly.

Tamir walked around the table and sat down beside her, smiling with his eyes like someone who couldn't get a joke out of his head. Ayelet grabbed his tan hand, and the two of them engaged in a playful tug of war until, finally, Tamir let go. He leaned back and watched her, quiet and mesmerized, as she held his arm before her blue eyes, playing with his thick, black rubber bracelet. She asked some questions about it, and they had an absurdly serious conversation about the nature of the bracelet. I listened, mystified.

Ayelet's parents strolled through, coffee cups in hand. They beamed at us, then followed my mother out onto the balcony, leaving the glass door open as they sat around a table in the sun. They conversed in low voices, surprising bursts of laughter dotting their exchange.

My friends recounted the goings-on at school, joyfully supporting and completing each other's sentences. But as I pictured the faces and places I knew so well, what stood out to me were only things that had changed.

Zohara lay staring at the ceiling, shrouded by worries about the complications her doctor had prophesied. I held her hand, but after an exhausting day of surveying a conservation building, I was too tired to offer any words of comfort. While I pictured those thick-walled rooms where diagonal sunbeams dispersed the dimness, I slipped softly into a deep sleep.

In my dream, I was going to the movies with Tamir and Ayelet. She was his date in the dream, though, in reality, she'd been my childhood girlfriend. The movie theater was at the top of a hill with a forested road leading to it. There were no seats inside. The audience stood for the entire film. My friends stood together while I stood on my own a few rows away—until the middle of the movie when Ayelet appeared before me as an adult woman and asked me to kiss her. I realized right away that she was only doing this to make Tamir jealous, but I still pounced at her with an aggressive passion, confused as to why she seemed to be trying to restrain me.

As we left the theater, we descended an archaeological mound between heavy stone walls, heading toward a grand archway. On our approach, I spotted a narrow opening at the base of the arch, right above my head, with a wooden crane hanging in front of it, equipped with two pulleys. I knew this was a cash register where people bought movie tickets, but I had no idea how it worked.

I climbed up a twisting stairway inside one of the pillars of this state-of-the-art archway, wriggling around until I reached the center of the hollow arch, then pushed my way through that narrow opening in the ground.

Then, the aesthetics of the dream changed, the tones softening. I saw myself sleeping on a narrow mattress. I was especially interested in the folds of the sheet around my body, the weight of which was dispersed equally along the mattress. I seemed to be sleeping well, and the sight soothed me momentarily. However, I soon realized that the sheets were tightening and stiffening beneath me, reminding me of the uncomfortable journey here. Suddenly, a strange feeling of lightness disturbed me. I reached for the burden of the bag that had long been on my shoulders, and as darkness crept in at the edges of my vision, I found myself retracing my steps in search of the lost bag.

I turned back into the theater, but rather than joining my friends, I headed to the lost and found, where an employee handed me an unfamiliar sky-blue bag full of binders. I shrugged off the surprise and hoisted it onto my shoulder. Just then, I was informed that my friends and I had to attend class immediately, but I'd already lost track of them. If that wasn't bad enough, my journey to the classroom became convoluted, twisting and turning through narrow pathways made of crumbling sandstone.

The next night, I had a similar dream: I was wandering through a foreign city, dawdling through odd alleyways, until finally, I walked into the foyer of a tall building. I learned I was renting an apartment there with a roommate, but I had no idea which apartment was ours.

Countless mailboxes dotted the wall before me, and I spotted an open one. I walked over and pulled out a shoelace with a key imprinted with the number 9. I caught its meaning and realized I was actually supposed to have apartment number 8.

I went to apartment 9, arranged my things in an available room, and left town. Upon my return, I discovered that my belongings were no longer in my room and that a new roommate had taken my place. Then I learned my former roommate and this new roommate had packed all my things in two large backpacks. I was furious, and a loud argument ensued between us. I would not back down nor share my room with this new person, but it was my former roommate who burst into tears first.

Five months or so had passed since the accident. My mother had embraced Sofia's frequent and warm invitations to live near her neighborhood in the city of Ra'anana, and we bid farewell to my grandmother's apartment. Thus, we never returned to our village home; I never saw it again, except once, years later, when I found the courage to drive by and catch a glimpse of its old Mediterranean-style façade.

Now, an armchair and a square couch of thick wooden planks that my father had crafted were set on the floor of a small apartment, three stories up, on the corner of Brenner Street in Ra'anana. Behind the back of the wooden couch was a long, dark row of leaning shutters. On the other side, a wild rain interrupted my mother mid-sentence. Plump drops reflected the twinkle of streetlamps, tapping nervously against the roofs of parked cars.

There wasn't enough light in the apartment; we were missing some bulbs. Mom sat in the armchair, warming her hands in front of a space heater, and waited patiently as I shifted my injured leg aside before ducking back down, closer to the radiant heat.

"I just couldn't… I couldn't picture myself living there alone, without your father. Do you understand? The memories, they…" She put her palms to her forehead and closed her eyes as if in pain. "They would be everywhere, and we would keep comparing it to our life before."

Our gaze met when she opened her eyes, but our separate worries thickened in the space between us, like breath on a cold windowpane. Mom pulled herself away from her reveries with a deep sigh and added, "Even here, where everything is new, whenever I set the table for dinner…" A stifled sob escaped her. The morose image her words painted crushed my heart. Her lower lip trembled, jutting out her face, and she looked like a baby holding back tears.

I remember her hands returning to the drawer an extra knife and fork she'd picked up out of habit, but I'm not convinced I actually saw this. Perhaps it was only a picture conjured by what she'd told me.

In my dreams, I returned to my village bedroom, sitting gloomily on my childhood bed, glancing at the soft dimness around me as if from behind thick glass, until my eyes adjusted to the light and could see the model airplanes I'd hung from the ceiling. Every second, I glimpsed other belongings that had remained intact, their whisper growing louder in my ears: "Not everything is ruined… not everything is ruined…" My spirit gained strength.

Ami descended from a wooden ladder and nodded. Mom flipped the switch. Blinding light washed over the living room, so sharp and pale that it left no room for shadows. The furniture seemed to be pushing against the walls for a moment, naked and slim. Later that gray Saturday evening, they moved among the rooms. In some, Ami installed new lamps; in others, he unscrewed delicate bulbs and inserted stronger wattage ones. When their work was complete, Ami drank some of my mother's coffee and chatted with her in the kitchen. The rest he downed while standing in the hallway.

Almost a week passed, but the smell of fresh paint still lingered in the air. Gaping cardboard boxes lay in a pile by the door. We had found places for most of our things, but the apartment still felt foreign to me. My mother's eyes would sail over the space, constantly examining and rearranging the knickknacks on the living-room shelves, hammering nails into patches of walls that seemed too bare to her, and hanging some adornment or picture on each.

At that time, only a couple of days remained before the screws were to be removed from my left leg. Following my mother's advice, I stayed home to start my time at the new school without them. It was a rather obvious choice, given that I had already missed approximately three months since my sixth-grade school year started. Meanwhile, in Sofia's company, my mother went to the city hall to run errands and familiarize herself with the nearby shops. From time to time, around the kitchen table, between sips of coffee, they would delve into conversations and recollections of my father. On occasions when my mother sobbed softly, Sofia would draw her chair closer and offer her a comforting embrace.

The screws in my leg still caused me pain and discomfort, but both my body and mind had grown fatigued and apathetic to these woes. So, the depth of my disappointment gradually surfaced in my consciousness after a red-bearded orthopedist examined my x-rays under a neon glow, voiced his concern to Ami, and informed me that I would need to keep the leg fixation for another six weeks.

Ami and I walked toward the car along an avenue of chinaberries between the parking lot and the satellite hospital buildings. The buildings were scattered among shaded lawns and connected by narrow concrete paths, a tranquil scene that made me yearn for our village home and the comfort of shelter.

The sun shone behind the autumnal treetops, glimmering with dust particles that covered the car's dashboard. It was warm, and Ami rolled up his sleeves, revealing more of his hairy arms, scarred from his welding work. I couldn't take my eyes off them, even when he took hold of the steering wheel and got the car moving, turning so the diagonal sunbeam shone against the right side of my face.

Ami flicked on the radio and listened to the newscast. I leaned my head against the cool window and narrowed my eyes until they lost their focus—the other cars and trees turning into swift spots of color. I slowly drowned in a vague sadness, and whenever my lids fluttered closed, loud visions took over my consciousness in a loop, repeating themselves repeatedly without forming any focused thought.

My mother's silhouette waited behind the third-floor shutters, retreating when Ami pulled the car up next to the sidewalk. He undid his seatbelt and, without killing the engine, stepped out and walked around to the trunk. After a brief moment, he approached my side and opened the door, setting the walker he'd pulled from the trunk before me. I got up behind it, held my head high, and saw my mother coming out, the lobby door slamming behind her. I walked around the hood of the car, and when we met on the sidewalk in front of the building, she dropped her arms and looked at me with melancholic eyes.

"Oh, son. You're disappointed."

I whispered that it was no big deal, while Mom came closer and knelt. Tilting her head, she rubbed my cheek, and I saw the sadness in her face.

"I just can't stand seeing you having a hard time," she said, her voice trembling, her tone seeming to beg for acknowledgment.

I murmured in agreement, fixing my eyes on the cracked pavement.

Mom touched my back, and we climbed up the gradient incline toward the building's parking lot. Ami walked us to the corner pillar, said goodbye, and then watched as we moved through the shadow of the elevated building to the tiled floor of the lobby.

That evening, we convened in Mom's bedroom. She got into bed and tucked herself into her yellow comforter, then shifted her long body underneath the blanket until it reached its regular spot on the left side of the bed, close to the chilly wall. I wondered if this came from the habit of many years or if it was a secret yearning that, under the cover of night, Dad would materialize to sleep by her side.

She raised the corner of the comforter in a wide arc. When she invited me to curl up with her, I felt physically uncomfortable. I lowered my eyes to the floor, muttered an excuse, and sat on the side of the bed. Together, we undressed a full-size chocolate bar from its formal outer wrapper and its underclothing of aluminum foil. Mom sucked on a chocolate cube, swallowed it down, and showered me with words meant to minimize the orthopedist's decision. At the same time, my disappointment was wordless, and my composure was merely a result of my fear of breaking down in front of her.

The lamp my mother switched on in the hallway every night before turning in reached a long finger of light all the way to my narrow bed. The words of comfort I'd heard that night, sitting on my mother's bed, did not sprout in my soul. Lying in the darkness of my room, I harbored a vague hope that Mom would delay my return to school, but the very next night, after a brief conversation, she pulled a bag of fresh stationery from the closet, wrapped some notebooks, and packed a book bag for me.

As was her way, she strode with despair-fearing optimism, and I followed, in my habit of matching the pace of my emotional processing with her mood, not daring to show any resistance.

In the dark, I held onto an extinguished torch resembling a broomstick with a spongy white cylinder at its end. I hurried down the stairwell of the building on Brenner Street, waving the torch from side to side as if to set fire to anything in my path. As I stepped onto the road, I discovered that the people circling me like shadows in my mother's apartment had paid no mind to my dramatic exit and didn't even bother to follow me outside. I was appalled by my own actions, and yet, there was a part of me that wished to give in to the madness that was taking over.

Furious, I returned to the apartment, where the same dark figures surrounded me again. I lit the torch before their eyes and burst out the door again, yelling. I ran down the dark stairwell and out onto the entry path, waving the torch and casting orange tongues of flame that burned fleshy plants on every side.

Zohara called my name over and over again.

When I opened my eyes, she said, "You were yelling."

I propped myself up on my elbows. From the corner of my eye, I caught her, removing her hand from my shoulder. I wondered if she'd been shaking me awake. "You're awake?" I asked.

"Have been for a while now. I can't feel him moving."

The images of burning greenery and the raised torch still floated before my eyes. "Are you worried?"

Zohara lay back down beside me, rubbing her plump stomach over the nightgown with an expression of concentration. I tried to catch her eyes, but her senses were entirely devoted to the goings-on in her uterus. A long time passed over me before Zohara snapped out of it, looking at me and blinking with confusion as if surprised by my presence. She ran the same gaze over our room, which was illuminated dully by the moonlight.

"Could you get me some chocolate?"

I got out of bed in my underwear.

"I'm probably just making a big deal out of nothing," she added.

I pulled on an undershirt. As I walked out of the room, I heard her whispering behind my back. "It's meant... to wake him up." I wasn't sure if she was directing her words at me or merely trying to reassure herself.

I pulled a bar of white chocolate from the top shelf of the cupboard. The torch from my dream, a broomstick with a spongy white cylinder at its end, reminded me of one of those cotton swabs that were used to sterilize my wounds, doused in the burning hydrogen peroxide. I unwrapped the chocolate bar and broke off a row of squares. The fridge roused in a humming that broke the silence. I returned the chocolate bar to its shelf and slammed shut the cabinet door when suddenly my mind slowed as I heard a whisper, just like the child's whisper I'd heard in the dimness of the bus.

I am not adept at conjuring up the voices of people who have departed from my life, but the one I heard now was clear and distinct and gave way to sensations that drew me to the window, then out to the yard, still holding on to the chocolate pieces that were softening in my hand. As the tails of those long-forgotten phrases escaped my awareness, fading away among the chirping of crickets.

—

An angry call came from our bedroom window. I couldn't say how much time had gone by, but I found myself standing barefoot on the thin grass, watching the bushes and shadows at the edge of the yard, toward which young Yaara had skipped away and vanished.

She appeared so real to me that, had I been fast enough, I could have touched the scrunched fabric of her waistband and the collar of her simple T-shirt, hemmed and faded from washing.

Back in the kitchen, I threw away what was left of the chocolate cubes and washed the white smudges from my hand. Then I broke off a new row and delivered it to Zohara in the bedroom, apologizing and excusing my delay with a story about a hedgehog I'd been watching in the yard.

But Zohara was too worried to listen, focusing her attention on the sugar she now sucked. She lay down on her left side, and when she placed a tentative hand on her belly and closed her eyes, I pictured that rotund, prickly hedgehog I'd made up.

She breathed superficially for a long time before a soft smile appeared on her lips. "He's moving," she whispered, then turned onto her back. Her body went limp as if having just endured a great effort.

The more haunted I became, the more my sanity dwindled. I grew methodical in my search. Young Yaara often visited my imagination, and I longed for those fantasies almost as much as I feared becoming swallowed by them. Encountering Yaara, the adult, a woman of flesh and blood who shared my memories of those long-lost days, took on in my mind the shape of an elixir that would cure these peculiar states of mind taking over me.

At the hospital, I looked over the metal plaque etched with the names of departments. It was already five o'clock, and visiting hours only lasted until eight. I planned to conduct a thorough search, but after less than an hour of wandering between the wards, a choke ring that seemed to find me whenever I entered a hospital began to tighten around my neck. The force of the storm of memories blowing through my mind, drawing my attention to pale faces in white beds, the rustle of a curtain drawn shut, and a few patients who were the same age as me, inching along the hallway, dragging IV stands with them, had me retreating down a dim stairwell back to the lobby.

I fed some coins into a vending machine, which rattled, spat out a disposable cup, and poured coffee into it. A security guard standing by the open door nodded at me as I passed him on my way out. I stood at the edge of a broad, elevated foyer that people climbed to on wide stairs from the yard. The Carmel wind blew on the back of my head and mussed the tops of trees, which gleamed in the early sunset. I took long, soothing breaths of the fresh air I so badly needed and sipped slowly on my hot beverage, the sweetness of which burned my throat.

Rather than acknowledge me with another nod, the security guard ignored me as I turned to go back inside. I lingered for a moment beyond the threshold, and the guard sighed wearily behind my back. Before me, a dark hallway stretched into a high-ceilinged lobby where I'd stood earlier, looking at the metal plaque. Now, the sunlight sliced the air with diagonal contrails. I took a decisive breath and walked on.

A nurse emerging from the emergency room with a determined step cut me off. She seemed familiar the instant I glimpsed her profile. With her chestnut-colored hair casually tied in a swinging ponytail, she perfectly embodied the carefree essence of the rural girl I longed for. As she moved away from me, walking tall, I could see the butterfly shape of her hips through her tight nurse's scrubs. Her torso had remained long, though her body had grown fuller, her noble posture unscathed. As she walked, she projected great power.

The nurse paused by the vending machine, her left leg stretched out in front of her, and chatted with a sturdy man in his fifties, wearing a surgeon's coat. I recognized the lilt of her voice, though the voice itself had grown hoarse over the years. Was she now a heavy smoker?

The surgeon handed her a steaming cup that emerged from the machine. She held it to her lips, sending the steam billowing when she blew on it. The surgeon, who had been rummaging through his plump wallet, now shoved it into a pocket in his blue scrubs, slipped a few coins into the slot, and they both waited in comfortable silence.

I was still leaning against the wall some distance away, holding onto the empty cup that had drawn my attention to the connection between me and Yaara. In a moment, the surgeon would pick up his own cup, and the power dynamic would change. Would the two of them pass me on their way back to the emergency room? Yaara's body language insinuated a parting, and indeed, when the surgeon had the cup held in his bearish hand, their paths diverged.

I closed the distance between us. In the elevator, Yaara stood with her back to me, hovering over a skinny man in a wheelchair, her pretty profile reflected in the mirror. Her adult life seemed so full and well-structured that it would never have occurred to her that I could be standing with her between those metal walls.

On the fourth floor, she stepped out of the elevator, and I followed her, quickening my steps.

I called her name in a dense whisper.

She turned her preoccupied face to me, and her expression changed instantly. "Oh, Gur. What are you doing here?" she said, and then hesitation flickered through her eyes. "Are you all right?"

"Yes, why?"

"People don't come here for no reason," she said, glancing at the sliding doors to her unit, which opened with a gust behind her back. An orderly was pushing a bed upon which a bony figure was covered from head to toe. My eyes followed the bed as it rolled away.

"Relax, he isn't dead."

"I know."

"Do you? Because for a second there, you had that same look you used to." Yaara ran her eyes over my face with a hint of a brash smile—a precious twinkle of her mischievous youth or the result of a sense of ownership she felt over me? She was wearing makeup, her face looking old in the neon light. The scent of her perfume mixed with the odors of sanitizer and medication. All in all, she appeared to have remained more steady on her feet than I ever was, having gained a unique resilience to go along with it all. Perhaps this was a power reserved for hospital nurses alone.

At that moment, a discomforting hush enveloped us, and I recalled one of the precious occasions when I had failed to seize Yaara's affection for me. Years ago, as we sat tightly squeezed on the red leather back seat of her father's car, returning from the movies, her adolescent body gradually shifted toward mine, and I still wonder if she was pretending to be slipping, when she leaned her head on my shoulder.

"What an extraordinary coincidence." Yaara's wistful sigh pulled me to the present, and for a fleeting second, I noticed her eyes rising with anticipation toward the hospital's acoustic ceiling.

"You know," I said, "It's quite rare for such positive things to occur," but upon hearing my own words, I felt a sense of remorse, and we both fell back into silence for a moment.

"Are you feeling okay?" she asked, gazing at me with a prolonged, penetrating stare as if seeking whether the fragility still resided within me.

"Yes, really," I said abruptly. Yet, my tone was tinged with a hint of defensiveness.

"Then, why are you here?"

"I'm just visiting. Didn't I mention that already?" I hastily responded, noticing her widening eyes. I felt a lump in my throat as I said, "A friend from work… his wife was due to give birth a… and…" My words faded away into silence.

"Don't you read signs anymore? Maternity is on the second floor," she pointed out.

Her gesture appeared so authoritarian to me, and I said lightly, "Well, now I'm really glad I bumped into you."

"Yeah… me too."

Her warm voice and the gentle curve of her smile charged me with the courage to ask her, quite friskily: "So, what kind of illness does one have to have for a chance to visit you?"

"Put it this way, I wouldn't advise it as a hangout place," she said, stealing a quick glance at the watch fastened to her chest pocket before letting out a heavy sigh. "Oh, what a day."

"If you live nearby," I told her, "the easy come and go might bring you some comfort after all the hard work." I strove to sound comforting and sure of myself, though I was left with a lingering feeling that Yaara's business demeanor concealed a delicate hint of sadness—or perhaps disillusionment—about me.

Before I could explore that suspicion further, Yaara responded, "Yes, right here in the Carmel. We've got an apartment with a view of the bay." She nodded lightly, but her cypress-green eyes told me her thoughts were elsewhere. Finally, she sighed and added, her voice morose, "My parents recently sold the apartment on Oliphant Street."

I nodded in sympathy for Yaara's dejection, which worsened the more details she shared with me about the sale, the renovation, and the demolition that would precede it. She elaborated on the news I'd already gathered about her in my investigation. I felt a hot flush spreading through my cheeks.

"Maybe," I said tentatively, "we could say goodbye to the apartment together?" I searched Yaara's face for the slightest twitch of recognition.

Zohara chose to leave me a note in the bedroom, under the beam of the nightlight, rather than on the ground at the entrance to the house, as was our custom.

It was as if she gained some kind of satisfaction from picturing me moving through the house, calling her name.

I picked up the note, walked into the dark living room, and dialed the number of her parents' house. Zohara picked up. At first, I felt relieved, but our conversation was brief, and silence enveloped me in its wake. I lumbered over to an orange pool of light that puddled on the bedroom floor, then returned to darkness, then back to light, and so forth, wandering and recounting a bit of our phone conversation in my mind.

"I see you didn't take the car. You want me to come over?" I asked.

"No, that's fine. I'm resting, and for now, everything is all right. Mom's here, and she's taking care of me," Zohara said in an indulgent, childish tone, which told me her mother was nearby, listening in. As I often did, I envisioned their twin expressions and twitches as they passed each other wordless messages during our call, and my spirits sank even lower. Zohara wasn't feeling well. She needed rest. I should've understood it, but from the labyrinth of my mind, I couldn't help but perceive her choice to stay with her parents as a sophisticated act of revenge against my growing fixation with Yaara.

I fell asleep sitting upright on the couch and woke up after midnight. The darkness around me was so thick that, for a moment, I wasn't sure I'd even opened my eyes. Gradually, sub-shades and dim forms came into view, and I recalled how, before falling asleep, I'd paced the house with balled fists, needing no light beyond the meek beam beside our bed.

A rice-paper lampshade dangled from the living room ceiling. When I turned it on, it shed a yellow light, murky and cumbersome on the eyes. It had been three and a half hours since Zohara had told me, "Don't worry, I'll call you if anything changes," by which statement she'd anchored me to the phone, which had since remained silent on the credenza. Besides this, there was the Peugeot keychain, threaded with the car keys, the house key, and another brass key, which was paired with some unknown lock.

My eyes moved from the keys to the phone. Dawn could break before it rang, I thought, yearning to return one last time to the two apartment buildings, sensing with all my might that in the enclosed, weedy yard, or perhaps in the public garden on Moriya Avenue, Yaara was waiting, her hair blowing in the cold wind, and I felt guilty for leaving her all alone in the thickening darkness.

I picked up the phone and made sure I got a dial tone. Then, I returned it to its cradle, allowing the click of the earpiece into the base to echo through the silence. I got up and went to the window, pulling up the blinds. The golden light from the room behind me and the darkness before me rendered horizontal bars through which I could look outside. Here, too, the wind blew through the trees, but it was most likely softer than the one that blew up on the Carmel. I threaded a hand between the blinds to feel the wind's caress on my fingertips.

I turned off the living room light. The elevated nightlight signaled to me, and I walked over to the edge of our bed, but the empty space in it startled me. I needed Zohara lying to my left, on the side of the bed, closer to the wall. And yet I wasn't thinking about her with tender longing, but rather with fury. She appeared in my mind, with her large pregnant belly, sleeping soundly in her childhood bed at her parents' home.

Mom once met a man who turned out to have known my father back in the seventies, when they both studied aeronautics together.

"This guy says, 'Of course I remember him,'" Mom told me, quoting him with pride. "'A handsome guy with a good head on his shoulders.'" To fan the spark of satisfaction in her eyes, she took a long inhale through her nose, straightening up against the backrest of her chair.

In my imagination, a black-and-white version of reality took form, in which my father lived the life of a young student. The impression that it wasn't death that had come between us but rather our placement along the timeline irritated my nerves. I agonized with a longing to be at my father's side, so much so that I lost interest in the routine of my days. I neglected my rented room, and the food rotted in the fridge. I skipped most of my classes at the Bezalel Academy of Art and Design, hardly handing in my assignments—which were sloppy at best.

At the rollicking Purim party, towards the middle of my third year, I stood on the sidelines. A girl in a Spiderwoman costume danced toward me. It was Zohara, as I'd learned a few hours later. "Why don't you join the fun?"

Lights flickered. Loudspeakers spewed music from all directions. "I think I have a fever," I said.

She looked at my face intently, got up on her tiptoes in her high boots, and put her lips to my forehead. "You're fine," she determined, her expression changing. "What's your costume?"

I put on my black hat and said, "A charcoal stick."

Zohara placed a hand on her hip, eyeing my basic costume, holding her gaze on me for so long that I felt embarrassed. Finally, she asked, "Why didn't you paint your face?"

I shrugged. A feverish chill ran down my back.

She had Spiderman radios hanging from a belt around her waist. She pulled one out and handed it to me. "Call if you get into trouble," she said. Then she turned away from me, raising her bare arm from the strap of the leotard, waving for a long time to make sure I watched her walk away. She found her girlfriends, and the three of them were swallowed into the bobbing crowd.

This wasn't the first time I'd noticed her. A week earlier, she cut me in line to join her friends who had been waiting to pay at the art supply store. A restless guy in blue coveralls who was waiting ahead of me shifted his weight from foot to foot, his curly hair and shoulder blades blocking the paleness of her sloping shoulders, whose vulnerability pulled at my heartstrings.

Mom steered our dilapidated Fiat through the busy parking lot of the school in Ra'anana as if battling against a malicious beast. Many minutes went by before she found a spot by the fence. She sighed and pulled on the handbrake, which replied with a choked, mechanical defeat.

I sat next to her, wearing a striped shirt she considered fancy, weak, and worried ahead of my introduction to my new classmates. The knowledge that in just a few minutes, I would be standing in my scarred mask before a classroom full of strange boys and girls mortified me, especially when I pictured the revolting expressions my appearance would inspire.

Mom sighed deeply. She was lost in a private stock-taking in front of her reflection in the rearview mirror. I watched her for a long moment, during which the essence of our pathetic estrangement in this city, in which we'd ended up under bad circumstances, solidified. But when she turned her face back to me, it no longer showed glumness but was charged with pep.

The hoarse school bell sawed through the cool November air. I hesitated, but then Mom walked around the car and opened the door for me. Next, she opened the back door and pulled out the walker, setting it before me. The bell's ringing died down, and the racket of the children followed suit. An imaginary lens, which had been distractedly following the crowd, now zeroed in on my bumbling march alongside my mother, forging a path for my walker through the dry dirt of the parking lot, which had been furrowed by rain into narrow, pebbly paths.

The bars of the gate and the fence surrounding the school were painted fresh green, a stark opposition to the severity of the school building—made of exposed concrete and resembling a fortress. As I came closer, I could only see the second story, peeking over the high fence, beyond which a thick hedge concealed the playground. An old security guard, who kept his eyes on us the entire way, now opened the gate with a gracious flourish, yet his politeness contained not a smile but rather the lowering of the head and the eyelids, as was customary in mourning rituals.

I took the stairs one at a time, my mother, the principal, and the school counselor following me in step. The principal apologized to my mother for placing me in a classroom on the second floor. She also explained that a girl from another homeroom had broken her foot in a skiing accident just two weeks earlier and that she and her classmates had taken over the last available room on the ground floor.

—

After six weeks of attending school, the fixation was finally removed from my leg. Two weeks later, after sanitizing and bandaging my wounds every day, I was walking without crutches. I was still exempt from gym class, so, while my classmates were exercising, I would wander through the yard alone, drawn mostly to hidden, bushy corners that reminded me of my old little school in the village.

Between the back of the gym and a bent fence and wild hedge, beyond which neglected tombstones dotted the rear of the municipal cemetery, I found a strip of reddish sand. These single graves, as well as the ones resembling marble double beds, were very shabby and derelict. I was drawn to them and started visiting them every time we had gym class. Soon after, I began to also visit them during the prolonged, embarrassingly lonely periods of recess. Ensconced in unripe and mostly unanalyzed sadness, I strolled along the bent fence and daydreamed.

On the weekends, Mom would pack a suitcase, and we would travel to Haifa. At my grandma's place there, I sought refuge from the many challenges I encountered at school. However, amidst the comfort I found, I couldn't help but sense the tense dynamic between my mother and grandmother, ready to erupt in every interaction between them. Despite this unease, we found ourselves returning there, weekend after weekend. I had my reasons to want to return, and as for my mother, I assumed she yearned for the affection and tenderness that Grandma could never wholly provide.

Mostly, my grandmother never lowered her eyes to meet mine, but she called me by a pet name and ruffled my hair. The one time she did look into my eyes, she praised me for resembling my father. Then, in a bizarre expression of affection, she squeezed my arm painfully, as if to offer intimacy and simultaneously warn me against it.

Now, Grandma ran her hand against the grain of my hair. "Don't you cut it?" she asked my mother.

Mom shrugged.

Grandma turned toward the kitchen, and Mom followed her. I heard Grandma pressing for details about my epilepsy and the meds I took. My mother's responses were vague to my ears, yet her voice carried concern and the sense of shame I always assumed she felt about me, given the ignominy my condition might bring. Gradually, their demeanor turned easy, and I sighed with silent relief as I heard them prattling and gossiping while they made coffee and walked out onto the balcony, which was being caressed by an evening breeze.

I stood against the railing and looked around. Yaara's bedroom window was wide open. Over the edge, like a long tongue, dangled a pink comforter that was being aired out. But inside the room, it was dark, and no light came on even as night descended. I imagined the family members all convened around the table for Friday night dinner, after which Yaara would go out with her friends—just as my classmates did.

—

Even then, I was haunted by an erroneous, yet persistent, assumption that the accident had derailed my life, sentencing me to an irreparable estrangement. Over the course of just a few months, I'd pulled away from my village friends, offering various excuses. I also stayed away from my classmates in the city until I was finally socially bankrupt. Walking alone through the schoolyard, I beat myself up for my embarrassing introversion, occasionally recalling, shamefully, how Ayelet had watched me slowly sitting down when she came to visit me at Grandma's house. The look she'd given me joined with the looks of my new classmates. Like theirs, it had made me feel that the sight of my injury and the knowledge of my father's death had cast a heavy shadow upon their innocence.

When I woke up, the cool sheets Mom had stretched over the couch the previous night were imbued with my body heat. The cooing of early morning doves and the languid tranquility of the streets were punctuated by the sounds of baking coming from Grandma's kitchen, forming a desert island in my mind's eye—a haven from the burden of the everyday.

I padded out to the balcony, noticing clouds gathering over the rooftops and the sky darkening. Shutters covered Yaara's window, but strips of light poked out from between the slats. A soft tapping sounded against the green leaves, and soon, a light rain started to come down.

The slats closed unexpectedly, the shutters pulled open with a noisy drag, and palms came out of the darkness within, turned upwards to catch the raindrops. As I watched, marveling, Yaara poked out her head and looked up at the sky.

A cry left my throat, "Yaara!"

She didn't hear me.

I mustered up my courage and shouted again, a silence-breaking shout, like the thwacking of rugs I'd heard from time to time during the many hours I'd spent lying, injured, on the couch.

Yaara waved at me lightly, cupped her damp hands around her mouth, and cried, "Come downstairs!" It was as if she always communicated in this way.

"I'm coming!" I replied, my voice breaking between words.

"Wait a minute. I'm in my pajamas."

"What?"

"Five minutes!"

I waved my hand and turned into the apartment.

I arrived in the building's lobby early. Impatient, I took the stairs down to the joint yard, and I waited for Yaara to emerge from her building at the end of the path. The rain had stopped, and only residual dripping sounded from plants or protuberances along building walls.

I was disappointed when Yaara was late, and even more disappointed when I saw the tiny dog that walked ahead of her, pulling on the leash between them. She walked with a forced bounce in her steps, wearing a ragged blue hoodie, shorts, and white sneakers with no socks. I was so thirsty for Yaara's attention that I was not magnanimous enough to share it, not even with a dog. And if that wasn't bad enough, whenever we paused to chat during our walk up the street and through the thin thicket alongside the Cinematheque,

Vachi would cling to Yaara's leg as if he were in heat. He lingered like this, tongue dangling out, for a long moment before Yaara noticed and shooed him off.

I left the Purim party long before it ended. Since I couldn't find the girl in the Spiderwoman costume, I kept the radio she had left with me. I moved away from the rumbling music to the cool darkness of Mount Scopus, carrying around a melancholy mixed with an odd satisfaction, while holding on to the antenna. It connected me to the girl's radio through frequencies that sent arousing chills through me, though no communication was coming through.

A streetlamp was the only source of light in my rental apartment. My roommate, who was studying for a respectable law degree, was a party boy and a much better fit than me for an art and design academy. He wasn't home, the door of his dark bedroom gaping open.

I swallowed a painkiller, washing it down with water from the bathroom faucet. Then, assuming a brief nap would suffice for me to recover, I lay down in my black clothes on my futon, placing the radio on the floor beside me. I stared at the spider-web design outlining the holes of the speaker, attentive to its ongoing rustle for a while, until I fell asleep.

A burst of broken exclamations emerged from the radio, waking me up. I had no idea who'd told her I lived in this neighborhood. After many repeated instructions and broken responses crackling through the roiling storm of frequencies, I gave her the address. Radio in hand, I looked at my face in the bathroom mirror, then ran, half-dreaming, to the doorway.

All of a sudden, the stairwell light came on, and the voice of the girl who had spoken to me over the radio echoed from the floor above.

"Down here!" I cried.

She descended toward me in her red-and-blue bodysuit, taking the careful steps of the intoxicated, almost losing her balance. "Whoa!" she called, grabbing onto the handrail with both hands, lowering her head, and giggling.

I took two steps up in her direction. She kept coming down. The closer we moved toward each other, the worse the screeching of our radios became.

My fifteen-year-old heart pounded with intensifying excitement with each stair I climbed. On the fourth floor, sounds of an argument came from the Grossbard apartment, masking my knocking on their door. It continued so long that after a while, I considered leaving. However, because I was so looking forward to meeting Yaara and seeing her reaction to my body, which had grown stronger and sturdier over the past year, I kept knocking with growing persistence.

Finally, Yaara opened the door and invited me straight to her room, in a hoarse voice that was atypically awkward. As we crossed the gap between her parents, I kept my eyes on her bare calves. The two adults stood in tense silence, and only her father nodded at me and muttered a greeting.

Yaara's cutoffs were teasingly short, which made me uncomfortable. The T-shirt she wore looked shabby, and her hair, undone and uncombed, added to the general impression that she hadn't been looking forward to my arrival as much as I had.

I dropped my backpack in the corner of the small room, and she asked about my long bus journey. I answered briefly, scanning my surroundings—the room of a fifteen-year-old girl who, just like her, wore a rebellious appearance.

Yaara invited me to sit on her wooden bed, which was slightly wider than a single and old-looking. Then she bent down and picked up a thick photo album from the floor. She sat to my left and leaned against the wall, opened the photo album, rested it against her crossed legs, and invited me to look. I leaned toward her as she flipped through the pages, peppering me with explanations.

The first few photos showed small groups of boys and girls in Youth Movement uniforms, their arms around each other, standing in the shadow of a bus, their friends in the background, loading sleeping bags and heavy hiking packs into the trunk. To my relief, these photos were rather general, as was how Yaara flitted over them, almost wordlessly, supporting the illusion I hoped to conserve, according to which Yaara's life, just like mine, has remained petrified between our meetings. But toward the middle of the album, in a series of photographs taken at Hexagon Pool, I saw a different Yaara.

Most memorable was a picture of her in a blue swimsuit that accentuated her beauty, huddling with a wet boy named Roi, a little shorter than her but with a mature face and rounded shoulders. They both barely kept their balance on the same narrow rock step. They must have plummeted into the greenish water only moments later, but in the brief moment caught by the camera, Yaara's long arms were spread open, and she was leaning back toward the boy in an acrobatic twist as he wrapped his arms around her waist like a harness.

She flipped the page slowly, a heavy mood descending upon her. On the next page, I could barely ascertain the orange hues that appeared in a series of photographs most likely taken in firelight before the album slammed shut.

Yaara sighed. "It's over anyway."

I looked up at her, puzzled. "What's over? The album?"

"No. It's my parents," she replied sharply. Then she held her eyes on the sunflower print on the cover and rubbed it gently with her thumb for a while before looking up and saying, "I know what you're thinking, Gur, but it's not that."

I looked at her.

She continued, "They suddenly got it into their heads that the Youth Movement is the reason I'm doing badly in math."

"How bad?"

"Worse than failing."

The playful tone in her voice pulled a smile out of me.

"But it isn't just that," she drew the words out. "Because I've also done a few other things that were… wrong." I thought I saw the hint of a satisfied smile on her lips or acceptance in her expression, and yet I enjoyed the subtle shift in our power dynamic. I was not about to reveal to Yaara that my grades were also bad, possibly worse than hers.

We sat in silence, our eyes meeting. I thought she wanted me to continue questioning her, especially about those things which she considered "wrong."

I recalled how, three years earlier, innocent Yaara waved at me from that window above her bed. I pictured her rising to her bare knees on the bed to get to the windowsill, and suddenly worried that the details I would soon find out would besmirch that image I had in my mind.

"What are you going to do?"

"Nothing, for now. They," she said, indicating toward the door, beyond which the sounds of another altercation wafted in as if just the mention of her parents awakened some curse that had been placed upon them, "won't let me go, and I don't think that's going to change."

Silence fell between us. My eyes scanned the walls, and when I focused on the blue Nirvana poster to the right of the closet, it was hard to pretend I couldn't hear the fight.

All of a sudden, fast footsteps sounded outside of the room, and a door slammed thunderously.

"Let's get out of here," she said.

—

Yaara shot a suspicious look at the path, making sure no one was following us. Then she sighed. "They're having a hard time again," she said, her tone pinching my heart. It made it hard to conjure the missing part of the sentence. I wondered if an easy time was even possible for parents who were so hostile toward each other.

The sun went down behind the mountain, and a gloomy sky spread over the roofs and the whispering treetops. From the edge of the path, we walked onto that abandoned lot, on the outskirts of which we'd stood a few years ago in awkward, wordless anticipation until her father arrived in his car to take us to the movies. Now, we crossed the street, and Yaara led me down a gradient slope, between building yards, while my mind stayed somewhere in my recollections of that car ride. Sometimes, I felt like a voyeur, watching real life from behind an invisible curtain, and the words and gestures I offered Yaara reached my consciousness after a brief respite.

"This way," she said. We crossed the shadow of a building along a low stone terrace and reached another concrete path. As we descended, I thought about how, since my childhood in the village, I had no intimate awareness of my living environment. Then I tried to mentally go through the route from there back to the abandoned lot, and from the lot to Yaara's building, but in the strange mood I was in, the assignment proved too challenging.

Yaara pointed toward the façade of an apartment building with an exterior staircase leading to the second floor. "That's where Alex lives. You can come with me. You'll wait outside," she added when she saw me hesitating.

I followed her up to the second floor, where she pressed the light switch. There, we ascended another two floors in an interior staircase dotted with glassless windows overlooking pine trees. An occasional wind blew.

Yaara entered the apartment without knocking, leaving the door ajar as she advanced inside. I sat down on one of the steps that continued to the next floor. The light over my head went out, and the stairwell was barely lit by the faint glow filtering out of the apartment. Alex's low voice emerged from inside, its cyclical melody reminiscent of the tired spins of a washing machine. But as carefully as I listened, I had trouble conceiving of the essence of their conversation. Was Yaara complaining about her parents while Alex consoled her? Or was he trying to persuade her to do so while she turned him down?

I looked around to make sure no one else was in the stairwell, then pushed the door a little more open with my foot. The hallway wall with its coat hanger blocked my view. A professional camera bag hung off it with a strap, exacerbating my curiosity. I wanted to widen the peeking space so I could glean more details, but approaching footfalls startled me, and I jumped back. I waited tensely for the sound to retreat, then angled a careful look and found that the camera bag had been removed from its hook.

Shortly thereafter, Yaara popped her head out and handed me a half-empty vodka bottle. She lingered at the top of the stairs. As she pulled her hair up, I noticed sweat beading on her forehead and the pungency of her breath.

"Shall we?" she urged me.

Perhaps she was upset to have me see her in such a fragile state, I thought, passing the cold bottle back to her. I did my best not to be insulted by her tone, and yet I quickened my step and got some distance between us. Occasionally, I heard the vodka burbling inside the bottle behind me and wondered if Yaara continued to take nips of it. A frightening thought entered my mind: with each sip of the drink, Yaara was pulling farther away from me, and soon, she would no longer be the one whose attention I coveted.

The smell of alcohol, the professional camera, and Alex, with the hypnotizing echo of his voice, and the sound of the tired spin of a washing machine, all melded together in my mind to form a scene of debauchery. My heart contracted with jealousy.

The yellow light went out again, and since we both ignored the next switch, darkness accompanied us down the last interior flight of stairs.

—

I paid no attention to our route until we sat down on a boulder on a slope carpeted with pine needles. It seemed we'd gained some distance from Alex's building, yet I was plagued by a fear that our complex journey among the buildings and woods had led us right into his line of vision.

"How old is this Alex person?" I asked, regretting the tone of disdain in my voice immediately.

"I don't know exactly. He's divorced."

"So, what are you doing together?"

Yaara tilted her outstretched foot until her flip-flop hung off her big toe, just above the bed of needles scattered here and there with broken bottles and cigarette butts. "Nothing," she muttered. "We just talk." As she spoke, she kept her eyes on her leg muscles, and I marveled at how slim and tight they were.

I recalled the camera that had been removed from the coat hanger. Meaningfully, I asked, "Is that all?" My heart was pounding, twisted with anticipation, as if yearning to hear Yaara convey details that would cause me turmoil and fan the flames of my fear of abandonment.

"He's a really smart guy, Alex. And he loves taking my picture," Yaara replied with defiant ease. She put her foot back on the ground, poured some vodka into her mouth, handed me the bottle with booze-filled cheeks, and then swallowed. She sighed, and as she folded her knees to her chest, lost in thought, I made a quick show of drinking without swallowing a single drop, then handed the bottle back.

She held the bottle's neck to her lips, looked at me, and said, "Don't worry, it's nothing perverse. He's a real photographer."

"I wasn't worried," I said quickly, but my body betrayed me. I felt certain this sort of relationship had to have a tragic aspect to it.

"Yeah, right."

"What?"

"Don't 'what' me. You're a bad liar."

She was right. Sometimes, my eyes truly were open windows to my soul. I hung my head and stared at Yaara's chiseled hand as she held the bottle to her chest. As I watched, I felt the ghost of her touch, as if breaking through the cover of years. As I'd done before, I indulged in it silently. When I glanced at Yaara without meaning to, she offered me a tender smile of grace.

I took a deep breath and asked her if she remembered that night at the movies. She kept her eyes on me the entire time and now nodded attentively. I swallowed and reminded her, working to steady my voice, of how then, under cover of dark, she had studied the scars on my face with her finger.

In the tense silence, before she responded, the fringes of my words seemed to return to my ears from far away, and the hairs on the back of my neck stood up as if we were still in that movie theater.

"Is that what you want from me?" she asked, her eyes widening with wonder. I watched as her face rode this new recognition into a sly smirk, at the end of which Yaara bit her lip. Without giving me an opportunity to respond, she pressed her hands into the boulder underneath her, raised her buttocks slightly, and shifted toward me. When she sat closer, my body bristled in anticipation of contact. Wordlessly, she brought her forehead to mine until I felt her eyelashes fluttering against my own. I inhaled her breath, warm and boozy, with pleasure, but before I knew it, she snatched her face away.

I blinked for a long moment, unsure what to do with my erection, as Yaara got to her feet. From the corner of my eye, I saw her moving away slowly. When I stood, she took another soft step along the needle carpet and paused to wait for me at the edge of the shadowed trees—the left side of her body gleamed in the light from a nearby apartment building.

The bottle lay on the ground, right in front of me, the dregs of liquid floating horizontally inside. I regretted not having dared to take a swig. Surely, it would have urged me to take action. The moment Yaara's lashes hovered over my eyelids, I should have taken hold of the back of her neck to prevent her from blowing away.

The closer I came to Yaara, the more she widened her steps, slipping away from me among the shadows of buildings and thick greenery. Then she burst into a run, flip-flops in hand—up the gradated path and back down it on the other side. I chased her into open yards, and there, in the dimness, just when I lost her and wondered which way to turn, the lightning bolt revealed her, reigniting the chase.

When we returned to the abandoned lot, my head felt dizzy again, the pace of my thoughts out of sync with the rhythm of my surroundings. My bizarre vision evaporated at once, and as relief washed over me, I dared not allow that sensation to return to my thoughts.

Yaara slowed down but maintained the atmosphere of the chase with mischievous zeal and a short but persistent space between us. She motioned toward the back of the lot and mentioned breathlessly that her father's car was not in its spot.

With effort, I closed the gap between us. She said her apartment would likely be tensely quiet until her father returned at dawn, agitated and on edge.

The apartment was stifling, the light dim. From the hallway, we could see our reflections in the balcony windowpane, trapped like ghosts between the dark glass and the drawn shutters.

Yaara kicked off her flip-flops in a wide arc, sending them flying to the middle of the living room. We smiled at each other when they whacked against the floor, still panting from running up the stairs.

I filled a glass of water in the derelict kitchen of my student pad and added some ice cubes. Out in the living room, I found Spiderwoman swaying on her feet, as if about to pass out. I offered her the water and asked her name.

She snatched the glass from my hands, took a long gulp, and replied, "Zohara," smiling vaguely. I offered to make her black coffee and give her a ride wherever she needed to go.

"Are you kicking me out?" she teased, grazing my shoulder.

"Never."

"So, can I spend the night… on the couch?" The cadence of her voice was the meandering music of the intoxicated.

I pulled the sheet off my bed. While I spread it over the couch, Zohara leaned one hand against the wall, and then used the tip of one shoe to remove the other. I went back to my room and returned with the rest of the bedding. I piled it on the end of the couch, and when I turned around, I was surprised to find Zohara directly in front of me, smaller than the image of her form that had fixed itself in my memory.

"Ugh! I can't breathe in this spandex!" Zohara groaned. She twisted her body toward me and undid a zipper in her suit, all the way from the nape of her neck to beneath her shoulder blades. Then she glanced at me. As she sat down on the couch, the fabric fell away from her, and her breasts peeked out.

I turned away, but from the corner of my eye, I could see that Zohara was in no rush to cover up—not even as she lay down and lazily pulled the blanket over her body. She looked at me and behaved as someone who was only partially there, or pretending to be.

I slept uneasily in my bedroom for an hour and awoke with feverish chills. The raincoat I was using as a comforter had slipped off; I pulled it over me again and curled up inside it. I shivered for a long time before sinking into a calm sleep, only to wake up minutes later.

Panicked, I jumped up, still lost in a fever dream in which my roommate came home with three drunk men who were now having their way with Zohara. I stepped out of the room, found her sleeping peacefully on the couch, and returned to my bed, dizzy.

At eight in the morning, I was relieved to see my roommate's door closed. I took two Tylenols, and by nine, when Zohara woke up with a hangover, I was recovered enough to conceal my sickness from her.

—

Zohara sat in the passenger seat, wearing a long cotton undershirt I'd given her over her costume. I drove while she leaned her head against the window, occasionally offering fatigued and hoarse directions to the Nachlaot neighborhood.

A deluge slammed down on the car in the narrow alleyways flanked by stone houses. I drove carefully, leaning close to the steaming windshield, while Zohara kept falling into brief sleep, as if assuming I already knew the way to her apartment building.

"There it is, right… there." Zohara popped up her head and pointed toward the widening at the edge of the alley we were driving down. She suggested I park there.

"Can you manage on your own?" I asked.

"You're welcome to come in. You should just know I'm not a pleasant patient." She giggled.

"Don't worry about that." I smiled back, then opened the door to validate my words.

"You're the one who should be worried." Her voice came out muffled from within the car. Then I saw the door opening and Zohara's towhead emerging.

Large windows framed with dark green metal opened out to an inner courtyard tiled with the same crude paving slabs that covered the entire ground floor, creating an impression of a loose demarcation between private and public. Zohara was afraid she might stumble and asked me to walk behind her up a narrow and twisting stairwell. On our way, she told me her roommate was visiting her parents. We walked by said roommate's bedroom and into Zohara's, which featured a double iron bed with cerulean linen, and a nook in the stone wall where a wooden plate served as a desk.

I contemplated the meaning of a postcard hanging above the desk, featuring a drawing of a naked girl standing in front of a mirror, rendered in angular, inky lines. I was mostly interested in the portrait of the artist, which appeared at the bottom of the image. As he drew the girl from behind, he included the reflection of his own face lowered above the canvas beside her double image.

"Here," Zohara surprised me by handing over my undershirt. "Hang on, I'm dying to take a shower."

"I'll be here," I said, dropping the undershirt on the bed.

Zohara walked away in her red-and-blue costume toward the ensuite bathroom. I hadn't even noticed it when I walked in, but now I realized I could easily watch Zohara showering behind that opaque glass door. I wondered if this occurred to her too, and decided to go wait in the living room.

The ruckus of the rain mixed in my mind with the sound of running water, though I doubted I could even hear it as I waited for Zohara in front of the window, watching ponderously as raindrops exploded against the circular slabs framing the house and the puddles forming in the cracks. A little time went by before I noticed Zohara's reflection among the golden lights that also appeared in the window, and I turned to face her.

She walked over in a white bathrobe, looked at me, then rose to her bare tiptoes, placed her light hands on my shoulders, and kissed me. I smelled her damp, clean hair. Then she retreated.

"You'll take me out to dinner when I feel better, won't you?" It sounded like a rhetorical question.

"I'd like that," I said.

Zohara smiled through tight lips and refastened her robe around her body. "You took good care of me, Gur," she said pleasantly. Then she hung her fair eyes on me and added, "I wouldn't have as much patience for someone I barely knew."

It was good to be in Yaara's room again. She leaned a knee against her bed and gave her face over to the chilly breeze that wafted through the open window. I squeezed beside her and leaned toward the window as well, as if it were the only source of oxygen. We were united once more. I glanced at her flushed cheeks that slowly lost their redness and felt an intimacy I had never known before.

Yaara went to find us something to eat. Upon her return, she sat beside me on the bed. We chatted easily as we munched on golden crackers dipped in a tub of cottage cheese that she held between us, until we finished the entire packet and wiped the greasy dust off our palms.

Yaara crushed the cracker packet into the empty cheese tub and placed it on the floor beside the bed. When she sat back up, she steered the conversation toward the topic of Alex. Mostly, she described his work as a traveling nature photographer, as if obligated to convince me of his professionalism. She'd first run into him walking around with his camera, kneeling, or even lying down on the ground to get a good shot. Her curiosity about him intensified before they even spoke. Once, without her knowledge, she became part of his composition—those were his words—and so he addressed her, asking her to remain in place for a moment longer, just like that, not move.

I didn't feel that any of this attested to Alex's true character, and I certainly wasn't reassured regarding the alcohol—surely compensation demanded from him, or the currency with which he paid her for a service she performed for him. Once more, I wondered about the tragic nature of their relationship and whether she was secretly in love with him, but I said nothing, afraid I might hurt her feelings or that my questions would be perceived as an admission of jealousy, diminishing the lovely spirit of friendship we had going.

Yaara left the room to brush the smell of alcohol from her teeth. In the meantime, following her offhanded instruction, I pulled the trundle bed out, its mattress covered with a shockingly loud floral-printed synthetic sheet. The bed was slightly lower than Yaara's, and it squeaked when I sat down on it.

When Yaara was finished, it was my turn to use the bathroom, so I grabbed my backpack from its resting place in the corner. Upon my return in pajamas, I found Yaara lying in bed, dressed in a nightgown.

I made the squeaky bed before lying down on my stomach. Yaara looked up with a tired smile, then fell asleep, her hand resting limply and slightly cupped in front of her face. I placed my hand over hers and closed my fingers around it as tenderly as I could. Listening to Yaara's breathing and feeling its gentle caress against my hand, I lost myself in slumber.

In the dead of night, we awoke as if in a strange dream. We searched for each other's bodies with curious, blind hands, soft and juicy kisses, and whispered moans of pleasure, until our inhibitions fell away.

—

I woke up with a heavy body and found myself in a hospital bed. An IV tube was pinned into the back of my left hand. Underneath it, my eyes were drawn to a dry bloodstain on my skin. I felt the caress of the sheet against my naked body and shuddered. I couldn't bear to raise my head from the pillow. Instead, I just turned it to the right.

Mom stood up from a nearby chair in simple house clothes. Her eyelids were heavy, and her smile was fuzzy. Dark treetops stood outside long windows, and a reserved sunlight lit up the room. Mom took my hand in hers, looked over my face, and shook her head with concern. "The doctors think it was another fit, but they're not worried," she said. Then, after a brief pause, she added, "Do you remember going to Yaara's yesterday?"

"Not really," I said meekly. From the corner of my eye, I spotted her sitting down just as I was letting my lids flutter closed, trying to concentrate. But this made me dizzy, and I gave up. I asked for the time.

"You've been sleeping for a long time. It's almost noon," she yawned. Then she gave me a long, worried look until finally she pulled on the shadow of a comforting smile and said, "Dalia said they panicked and called an ambulance. You know me. Just hearing her voice on the phone made me lose my mind. I drove like a madwoman. I didn't even comb my hair." She ran her hand through her frizzy hair. "You probably would have preferred your mother with her hair combed, huh?" she smiled.

I nodded heavily, but my mind was on Yaara. I was embarrassed to have her see me writhing around in an epileptic fit. My neck hurt, and I rested my head against the pillow again.

"Close your eyes," Mom whispered. "You still look a little discombobulated." Then she leaned back in her chair.

—

A neurologist looked over the scan and my test results and concluded that the scar in my brain was still causing seizures.

"But why now?" my disheveled mother insisted. Offhand, the doctor estimated that I either hadn't taken my daily dose of medication or had engaged in strenuous physical activity.

As he walked out, Mom called, "Excuse me, doctor…"

He popped his furrowed forehead through the curtain, raised his brows attentively, and answered that I would receive his discharge letter in an hour or two.

In the car, Mom gripped the top of the steering wheel alertly, driving with her head leaned forward and her eyes puffy from sleeplessness. We exchanged a few words, which slowly absorbed into the thickening silence. The more it thickened, the worse the discomfort I felt with my mother became, because whenever she was silent, I felt the same persistent guilt that could not be appeased with logic.

In the meantime, we left the twisting road descending from the Carmel behind us and kept driving south as darkness stretched above us and along the coastline.

"We'll be home in an hour. You'll wash off the hospital smell, and tomorrow we'll wake up like new," she said warmly, as if embracing me with her words. All I managed was a weak "yes." A different, meek tone had snuck into my mother's voice, a testament to the fact that she was hiding a concern from me—something she herself was uncomfortable with—and so she wished to wipe away its tracks from her memory.

I, on the other hand, through the force of my curiosity and other motivations bordering on self-cruelty, longed to peel away the scab from the wounds of my memory and return to the period of time I'd lost during the seizure. But all my efforts came back empty.

That night, I lay in bed looking at the ceiling of my room, wondering if the previous night's events had been wiped fully from my memory or if, one day, the details would return, like the shards of a shipwreck carried back to shore.

—

Mom passed me the phone. I held it to my ear, and Yaara asked how I was doing. I heard embarrassment in her voice and pictured her standing up and speaking into the turtle-green phone that hung from the hall wall, while Dalia, who had just finished talking to my mother, listened in.

My imagination housed the episode that had become lost in my memory among other fictitious visions that shamed me, and Yaara sounded distant on the phone. Each of us, in turn, dipped meager words into the flow of white noise until the conversation died on its own. Had I been able to conjure even a hint of the panic Yaara must have felt as I writhed in her bed, my heart would have gone out to her. But I was too eager and awed to envision that archived moment when the apex of our intimacy had risen and collapsed.

—

Ever since that cursed night, the months of Yaara's silence passed with the languorousness of years. The more they multiplied, the more I imagined her dislike for me growing—not because of anything she did, but because that was my way of interpreting silence. As I went to and from school, sounds and sights that I encountered recalled a vanishing sensation, weakening my spirit before I was able to get to the bottom of it— be it regret, a missed opportunity, or a bitter longing for that flash in time when I believed I was worthy of Yaara. With a hint of self-ridicule, I reminisced on how, the last time I saw her, I was captivated by a growing sense of strength, eager to exhibit it to her before disaster had reshuffled the cards.

When the phone rang, our apartment was ensconced in the melancholy of dusk. I wasn't going to pick up, but the tapping of my mother's knife against the cutting board in the kitchen did not relent, and finally, I got up from the couch. I held the phone to my ear and said hello, then recognized Yaara's voice searching for me on the other end of the line. She asked if she could speak to Gur.

She was surprised when I identified myself, paused for a moment, then said, "Oh, Gur, how are you?" Her tone did not invite an honest response.

"Fine," I said. "Long time no—"

"Yes," she cut me off, then fell silent, this time for a long moment that cast the shadow of the weight that had burdened our previous conversation. "I wanted to tell you," Yaara began, more energetically this time, and went on to explain that she'd transferred to an agricultural boarding school in the Moshav of Nahalal. I thanked her silently for the bridge she'd built over my awkwardness. I asked some follow-up questions, and Yaara's voice had already softened. And toward the end of the conversation, she invited me to come visit her at school.

—

Years later, I expected Yaara to wait for me in the lobby of the building on Oliphant Street, having pictured us walking up the stairs together and entering the apartment to share in a slow discovery of the details of the past—those that had survived intact. But in the shared yard, I was welcomed by a pair of wide slides made up of orange plastic links. Broken bricks spilled out through them from an open window on the third floor, sliding and landing one at a time, in a racket of demolition and flying dust, into a large metal container full of construction waste.

In the apartment, I found Yaara standing with her back to the door. Her arm was bent, and I imagined she was covering her mouth with her hand as she watched the rubble around her, stupefied.

The pounding of heavy hammers and the shattering of bricks rolled in from the back of the apartment, along with dust that rose on the light breeze blowing through the breached windows. In the tumult that brought to mind the teeth of time, I approached Yaara without her noticing and patted her shoulder. She turned halfway toward me, as if she'd been equal parts prepared for my arrival and eager to lose herself in her thoughts, with my presence a negligible bother.

She stretched up her neck with an inhale. "I'm taking this whole scene harder than I'd expected."

There was embarrassment in her voice. I looked at her as she ran her eyes over the destruction, lingering lengthily on the contours of broken bricks all the way to the plane of the floor that signified the boundaries of her brother's bedroom.

"We're too late," I said, nodding heavily. I wondered if Yaara was wiping tears away or only dust, which had been bothering me as well. We remained silent while three construction workers put down their tools and began chatting and saying their goodbyes.

"I guess the sentiments never go away," Yaara said, surprising me. There was longing in her voice, but I associated the word "sentiments" with estrangement, an emotional distance from the past.

I swept my arm behind her back. She looked at me askance. Carefully, I placed my hand between her shoulder blades, rubbing in circles. The light touch of her vertebrae, protruding through the fabric of her shirt, made me recoil. Though I continued to rub her back, it was as if a thin gap of air separated my hand from her body.

"And you remained as fearful as you always were," she said.

"Fearful?" I flushed with shame, my hand retreating of its own accord.

"When we were kids," she said. "I never knew how to put what I felt into words. But now I see you need a woman to take care of you all the time. As if you're still injured."

I lowered my head, a little hurt, but not fully fathoming her meaning. Most of all, I was worried that Yaara was about to open her heart and reveal to me the events of that awful night when I had a seizure in her room, spicing up the story with a medical point of view that would spare no details. My mouth dried up, and all the things I'd yearned to tell her before she started talking fell away.

Yaara glanced at her watch, a masculine Casio, and let out a bitter giggle. "I thought I'd never see you again," she said, "and now I'm sad to think that all of our encounters were brief and superficial..."

I suggested we go sit on the steps outside. "That's a nice idea," she said, "but Shlomi is going to be here to pick me up any minute."

I looked up. She was still examining me. Persuasively, drawing on her words, she invited me to come over to her place the next night, Thursday, around nine. She promised we would be completely alone. Then she bit her lip with anticipation. I wondered if I'd truly lived on in her memory as such a mentally unstable individual that she never imagined I might be married. But in that precious moment, in the apartment where darkness began to fall around us, Yaara was, to me, once again, that girl whose company I craved. I jumped at the invitation.

She gave me her address. I closed my eyes and whispered it to myself three times, committing it to memory, like a child.

Yaara smiled warmly. "Come on, let's go downstairs." As we walked out the door, she said, "I'm glad I ran into you," giving my shoulder a little nudge. "I would never have come here on my own."

In the distance, we heard the sound of an engine approaching from the direction of the abandoned lot. I said goodbye to Yaara before the twist in the path, before stepping out of the darkness and into the beam of the jeep's headlights.

I stared at her, walking tall, away from me, and asked myself how she was going to explain the reason for her visit to her husband. The car door slammed with that soft thud that nice cars make, and soon, its motor rumbled deeply as it made a sharp U-turn, dust rising in taillights.

—

The ringing of the phone preceded my entrance. I picked it up and heard Zohara's mother saying, "That's the thing, the doctor here is worried she might be entering premature labor."

I felt as if I'd stumbled into the middle of a conversation not meant for me. My palm on the smooth phone grew damp and warm with sweat even before Debbie deigned to acknowledge my existence on the other end of the line, before she recounted the bitter chain of events that had led Zohara to be rushed to the maternity ward, three and a half months before her due date.

Debbie sighed heavily. Then, over a detail-laden minute, she described the agony endured by "Zori," first as if trying to pull me out of my petrification, then explicitly urging me to get to the hospital.

Once I placed the phone back in its cradle, these events took on an unreal air, as if they had nothing to do with my own existence. An image breached my consciousness: Zohara giving birth to a living human being who would wrap its arms around my neck, its eyes searching for a father in mine. I wiped my sweaty palms on my pants over and over again, but they would not dry.

Then, a sudden panic hit me: I would miss my next day's meeting with Yaara. At once, my efforts to ignite the emotions expected of a newlywed and a would-be father were put out. And so, as I was about to leave, I called my mother to inform her of the birth—but even the heat of her voice did not inflame the desired feeling in me.

—

I identified myself at the nurses' station. A young, bony nurse generously offered me a baby-blue robe made of stiff, cold fabric. I slipped it on over my clothes, and she began to address me as "Dad." I wanted her to take me to Zohara, but instead, a stocky nurse stepped out from behind the desk, her entire being speaking of seniority and stability. She led me to delivery room number 6.

Throaty screams of agony broke through from behind closed doors, their intensity wiping away any identifying marks in the voices of the birthing women. But among the myriad howls of pain, I recognized Zohara's—within, her primal scream pierced through the whitewashed walls. In an instant, its painful trajectory morphed so drastically that it seemed as if the voices of three women derived from Zohara's throat. Amidst its dissolution, a trembling wail followed by a soft murmur arose, and then a pause, rendering Zohara's tone childlike and utterly reliant.

Abruptly, a shiver of the hospital's chill ran down my spine. Instead of surrendering myself to the demand to lean my hand on the corridor wall, I quickened my steps and followed the nurse into the room.

The wide back of a bull-like aging man in a surgeon's coat, and a young, briskly moving nurse, hid my wife from view. Across the way from them, by the head of the bed, Debbie's blond hair sporadically peeked out, too short and preoccupied to notice me. I wondered if I should present myself to the medical staff as the father and come nearer to Zohara, or use the prevailing circumstances to slip out. Before I could act, the nurse shot me a casual look and impatiently instructed me to take a spot by Zohara's head.

As the obstetrician moved between Zohara's spread legs, her tortured body revealed itself to me. A hospital gown was rolled up to her neck. Her pale skin had turned pink, like the inside of a clam, and a long trickle of sweat rolled down the wide space between her breasts.

Terrified, I spoke her name. She angled soft-focused eyes at me, and then her lids closed with an exhaustion that appeared absolute. A moment later, she let out a sharp cry and gripped her mother's hand with ferocious force. Her mother gave me an accusatory glare, stroking her daughter's hair, which had grown dark with sweat and clung to her flushed forehead.

With every passing minute, the doctor grew more agitated. I noticed sweat beading on his hairline as he spewed curt, worried instructions at the nurse. I put my hand on Zohara's warm arm. In the seconds she bit her lips and panted, I spoke softly to her. But whenever she experienced a bit of relief from the pain, the touch of her skin made me feel strange: it reminded me of the brief contact my hand had made with Yaara's back and how, feeling the shape of her spine, I had recoiled from that intimacy.

Zohara was weakening before my eyes, her lids drooping and vital machines beeping hysterically. The nurse commanded us to leave the room. In our wake, two severe-looking doctors stormed in, the youngest of the two almost crashing into me in the doorway.

Debbie remained by the closed door while I moved away slowly, plopping down, exhausted, on a perforated metal bench in the lobby of the labor and delivery ward.

Acknowledgment

I would like to convey my profound appreciation to my editor, Victoria Heath Silk, whose remarkable expertise, meticulous attention to detail, and exceptional grasp of the author's essence have left an indelible mark.